Glen Gair

Glen Gair

A Tale From A Highland Glen

Bert Scorgie

To order additional copies of this book, contact:
Xlibris Corporation
0-800-644-6988
www.xlibrispublishing.co.uk
Orders@xlibrispublishing.co.uk
303775

CONTENTS

Glen Gair is a typical Highland Glen, thirty miles long, about a mile wide, as is common in the Glens they have a good sized river running along the floor. This was just the ideal area to Construct a Hydro Electric Scheme. In the early fifties it was announced that Glen Gair would be the next site chosen by The Hydro Board to Construct their latest development. No doubt there was great jubilation among the Glen Folk, they could look forward to a bit of a Klondike over the next seven years. The first thing to happen would be the construction of two Work Camps with enough room to house roughly seven hundred men. The middle aged local guys stayed with their original employers probably because they were set in their ways, the few Estate workers that were still employed by the Laird would be worried if they left they would be letting the old Colonel down, so it was up to the younger generation to go for the huge wages being offerd at the Scheme. For the next seven years everybody was happy with their lot, but all good things come to an end, circumstances change, modern technology moves systems forward, not always for the best. Read my story and you will find out how things panned out in the Glens after the Hydro. Many of the characters in this book were//are real people with their identy changed. Quite a few of the incidents actually happened.

1

FOREWORD

Two years after the Second World War ended, the North Of Scotland Hydro Electric Board embarked on a huge Construction Programme. The aim was to harness the abundant free water available in the Scottish Highlands, one of the early sites was Glen Affric. Two huge dams were Constructed at Beinn—a—Mheadhoin in Glen Affric and Mullardoch in Glen Cannich. The purpose of these Dams was to feed water to the turbines in the huge Power Station at Fasnakyle (the biggest power station in the world at the time of Construction). A large Work Camp was Constructed in the village to house the five hundred Multi National Work Force.

This Construction Programme lasted from the late Forties until the early seventies when the last Hydro Scheme was built at Foyers above Loch Ness. With all the supposedly cheap Oil and Gas found in the North Sea, Hydro Power was deemed too expensive. During the twenty five years that the Hydro Construction Programme was active millions of pounds were spent all over the Highlands two of the Glens I am familiar with are Glengarry and GlenMoriston their likeness is quite coincidental. At the mouth of the river you have a small village, population probably less than two hundred. Driving through the village's you would never know that fifty years ago these villages were the center of huge Construction Sites, take Invermoriston as an example. You are driving on the road to Skye, three miles from the village you are confronted by a medium sized Dam, the main road travels up the side of the dam, it looks all rather insignificant. But with your eyes locked on the Dam I bet you missed the Tunnel on the opposite side of the road,the entrance to a huge under

ground cavern which houses the Power Station. Travel on for another two
or three hundred meteres and you come to a bridge, on your right hand side
you should see a sign saying Levishie Power Station, go on tell me you cant
see anything. Correct this road way leads you to yet another Tunnel which
is the main access to the cavern that houses yet another Power Station part
of a five million pound scheme built by A.M.Carmicheal of Edinburgh
around nineteen sixty.

As you drove up the main road you crossed over the Leveshie Tailrace
but you would not have noticed as it is underground many feet below, the
Tailrace by the way is like the waste pipe of your kitchen sink is allows the
used water to move on to the next phase. The Leveshie Power Station is fed
from a dam a mile up the hill through yet another tunnel eight feet by eight
it is a sloping tunnel, something like one in six so it was known as the Slope
Shaft, at the top end of this Tunnel is a fairly high Dam where the water is
stored until needed to drive the Turbines. Feeding the dam is yet another
mile long tunnel then a gap of thirty meters and you join up with another
three mile long tunnel that collects all the out lying lochs and streams and
channels the water to the dam, from the Power Station to the farthest out
tunnel is approximately seven miles, a fairly large Scheme but very little of
it seen from the main road.

As you keep heading West you come to Ceann-a-croc, on the right hand
side deep underground you have another Power Station this is powered
with water from the Loch Cluanie/Loch Loyne reservoirs. The statistics for
the Cluanie Dam are two thousand two hundred and fourteeen feet wide,
one hundred and thirty one feet high, it holds back millions of gallons of
water. The three combined Glenmoriston Schemes would have cost in the
region of twenty million pounds when constructed, to-day it would be
nearer two hundred million. This is just to give the reader an insight to the
amount of Concrete Structures that are hidden under the Highland Glens
and don't really disfigure our beautiful landscape.

My story is of how life would have been before and after the Hydro
Board had brought wealth and employment to the Glens. Glen Gair would
be a quiet backwater that just ambled through life living from hand to
mouth as the wages paid by the Estate and the Forestry Commision would

have been very basic. There would have been great rejoicing when it was announced that the next Hydro Scheme was being Constructed in Glen Gair. I have based my tale on things that really did happen in that era for example the story about the Copper Beech is practically true and the tree still stands on its original site so you could say my tale is based on fact.

One sad factor about the Companies that built these magnificent pieces of Scottish Engineering is that very few of them are still in business. I know for a fact that A.M Carmicheal and Duncan Logan Muir-of-Ord no longer exists. The Mitchell Construction Company who built the Cluanie Scheme also went into receivership many years ago. But may be back in business.

THE GLEN

Glen Gair is a typical Highland Glen, thirty miles long running from East to West, as is the norm there was quite a good sized river running along the floor of the Glen. The Glen was owned by various Society families, the major owner being Lt Colonel Mellis MM (retd), he had been decorated in the first world war for some sort of heroism he had performed at the Battle of the Somme. Mellis ruled his empire with a fairly strict set of rules, his loyal subjects looked up to him like he was some sort of god, they had no other option as he owned everything on the North Bank of the river, including all the small cottages occupied by his estate workers. On the South Bank there was a fertile swathe of land along which were dotted small crofts, behind this there was a huge area of common grazing where the crofters could graze their animals all summer. The South side was owned by the Forestry Commission, the ten crofters worked for the Commission and paid them rent for the use of the ground. Along the North bank there was an Hotel, Church of Scotland and a Shop/ Post Office, in between these buildings there was the Estate workers little cottages, very basic with only a fire place for heating and cooking, all situated in the living room, a sitting room and three bedrooms, the lavatory was a wooden shed with a big galvanised bucket, water was drawn from a natural spring further up the hill, there were no fancy frills just the basics needed for survival, lighting was by Tilly lamp and there was an abundance of wood to keep the fires burning.

The First World War had ended in nineteen eighteen which was seventeen years ago, the legacy of that conflict could be noted on the recently erected War Memorial upon which twelve names were engraved, the cream of the young men of Glen Gair, one of the names was that of the Lairds brother killed in action in Flanders, also, at least three men had suffered from gassing and shell shock, a legacy that would be with them forever, only their close families knew how badly affected they had been, constantly suffering nightmares and ill health, nothing was done to help them except when they became unmanageable they were shipped off and dumped in an Asylum.

Nothing exciting ever happened in the Glen, the retired Army Captain who leased the hotel from the Estate had built a wooden shed away from the main building where the local men could spend their wages on the demon drink, his idea was to keep the riff raff away from his precious guests who paid big bucks for the privilege of shooting Red Deer or to fish for Salmon in the well stocked river. Friday and Saturday night was the preferred drinking session evenings for the local men, most would leave at closing time well oiled, they were usually very subdued but occasionally old wounds would be opened up resulting in fisty cuffs, if it was serious the local bobby would be called upon, he would soon have everybody under control, quite often the two opponents would leave arms around each other, one telling the other what a great guy he was.

Occasionally one of the local girls would fall pregnant this was always a major issue, the parents after failing to persuade the young couple to do the decent thing and get married would huckle the wayward young lady away to live with relatives where nobody would know her, sometimes the baby would be kept and brought up not really knowing who its mother was at other times they would be put up for adoption, but it kept the gossip mongers in business.

One rather unique oddity in the Glen was the number of bachelors, sometimes two or three in the one family, the ones that did get married seemed to be quite well on in years before they decided to take the plunge, maybe the ratio was more men than women, also the fact that people didn't travel much then as the transport system was rather pre historic and many of the families were related.

Another unique feature of the Glen was that even though there was only a population of about two hundred there were three Churches. Church of Scotland, Free Church and the Roman Catholic Chapel, the C of S had the largest congregation followed by the Free Church, taking up the rear was the very sparse Catholic Congregation. As in every walk of life the religious divide is always present none more so than in Glen Gair although there was never any visible signs of animosity, under the surface the divide was present, the Free Church didn't trust the Catholics and the Church Of Scotland didn't trust either of the others although they all lived side by side in very near perfect harmony.

The mid thirties was a very hard part of the century everything was scarce none more so than money, neither the Forestry nor the Estate paid very high wages so it was always a struggle for the Glen folks to make ends meet, most of the people kept a few hens and possibly ducks, two or three sheep and some of them had a goat from which they would get milk. Of course even though the Laird was a very revered man who kept his loyal subjects under control, if the opportunity arose to poach a deer, a Salmon or a pheasant belonging to him it was taken, a way of supplementing the meagre diet found in most of the little estate cottages. He did allow the men to help themselves to fire wood from the hill and slabs from the Estate Sawmill, so there were opportunities for them to help themselves legally.

The village at the head of the Glen was the main populated area, but there were families scattered along the way most of them employed on the smaller estates and shooting lodges that made up the Glen after leaving the Mellis estate. It was a pretty bleak existence with poor road structure and public transport virtually unheard of, most of the Estates and Lodges had motorised transport so the housewives and housekeepers would manage a trip to the shop all be it maybe once a month, supplemented by the mobile shops that visited at least once a week. Most of the places would keep a few cows so that fresh milk was readily available, butter and cheese would be produced so apart from the loneliness it was probably quite a good standard of living.

THE INHABITANTS

The most important man in the glen has already been mentioned Col Mellis the laird and owner of the Estate, it had been in his family for years and was a thriving business, without the Estate Glen Gair would probably be a barren waste. The Laird had two sons both were following the family tradition and were commissioned officers in the Army one a Cameron Highlander the other was Royal Horse Artillery. The only daughter was at a boarding school where she would no doubt be being groomed to become a debutant in the near future. The next most important resident was a toss up between the manager of the local shop, the C of S minister or the Headmaster they were all important people in the welfare of the Glen. Another important person who helped keep the place running was the local contractor he had moved to the Glen from Caithness to work on the construction of the Inverness to Ft William road, he had struck it lucky when a house on the outskirts of the village became vacant and he was awarded the tenancy, he moved his wife and six bairns from near Wick and set up a small contracting business, his early days saw him carrying out the work using a horse and cart, Archie Cormack was a rough tough customer, a man who called a spade a spade. The man who managed the shop was from the East Coast, he was Bill Keith to name, his wife Wilma ran the Post Office, they were very much involved in community affairs and stringent Church Of Scotland members. Murdo Macsween a case hardened Islander was the head master, who along with his assistants did their very best to teach the bairns the latest curriculum available at that time. The Reverend Hugh McDade was the C Of S minister and a great servant to the community he worked tirelessly carrying out duties well above what was expected of him. There was a whole host of other people all carrying out essential tasks to keep the Glen ticking over, the estate Joiner, the District Nurse, the Blacksmith and of course the man who ran the Hotel, he was a retired Army man went by the name of Captain Blunt, he was a major employer as far as the ladies were concerned always employing plenty staff to keep the hotel running smoothly.

Then there was Donald MacLeod a native Glen Gair man, Donald had just recently returned to his native Glen having spent the last ten years on the Isle of Lewis where he was employed as head Game Keeper on a Sporting Estate. He was more or less forced to return home as both his parents now in their Eighties were unable to look after themselves even although they had two bachelor sons staying at home. Donald had married a Lewis girl, Mhari, they had three of a family, Mhari was heavily pregnant with their fourth child. Donald was a deeply religious man who followed his Free Church beliefs to the letter, it was possibly his beliefs that helped steer him through the turmoil that he faced on his return home. Both his brothers, Hamish at forty and Dougal at thirty eight lived at home they were hard drinking men who had very little idea how to look after elderly parents, most week-ends would see them drunk and then spending the pub closing times in their beds, they both worked for the Estate as Gamekeepers. Donald and Mhari had their hands full as they struggled to get things ship shape. The little cottage was bursting at the seems and of course there were no facilities as we know them in modern times, Mhari had her work cut out, luckily Donald didn't have a job so he was at home for a few weeks.

HOW IT ALL TURNED OUT

Life in the Glen just ambled on Mhari gave birth to her fourth child, a son, with the help of her neighbours she was able to struggle through. Donald's parents both passed away with-in a year, Mhari and Donald were sad to see them go but the relief must have been overwhelming, even with the help they had received it was still a hard way of life, with Donald's brothers still living in the cottage it was very over crowded. But the options were limited the only reason they had the cottage was because the two brothers were Estate workers this entitled them to a free house, part of the perquisites of their employment, anyhow Donald had his religious beliefs which were of great comfort to him, because of this he was able to put up with the way his wayward brothers behaved not that they were bad men more a case of being thoughtless. Boredom would maybe be another contributing factor coupled with the lack of funds, after one evening in the pub then having to pay digs there was not a lot left in the pay packet come Monday morning, enough to buy tobacco until the next pay day.

Nineteen Thirty Nine started off like previous years snow on the ground and not a lot happening. Then there started to be rumblings, there was unrest in Europe and the Germans were throwing their weight about. The Heads of State were trying their best to stave off armed conflict, many of the older Generation had clear memories of what had happened twenty years previous when the whole of Europe fought the First World War, causing millions of un-necessary deaths, no, War must be avoided at all costs. But avoided was not to be as Hitler was determined to show the world what a great guy he was and had delusions of the Germans ruling the world.

So on the third of September nineteen thirty nine Hitler's troops invaded Poland just the trigger needed to start a Second World War. Hitler was given a deadline to cease all hostilities and withdraw his forces otherwise the British and French would back the Poles and declare war on Germany, troubled times. As Britain waited with baited breath the deadline passed ,they had no option but to carry out the threat of Declaring War on the Hitler led Germans. The folks in Glen Gair had followed the happenings with great interest, many of the young men were in the Territorial Army, they were well aware that they would be called up as soon as they were required. Hamish Macleod was a gallus sort of character, he was at the forefront of the band shouting lets get stuck into them, but he had a bit of a problem if they were called up he was two years over the age limit, but he was sure that when he had filled in his T.A application form he had made out he was two years younger than he really was, it would be a blow to Hamish if his age went against him.

They didn't have long to wait before the King Requested their services, Mhari was busy doing the weekly wash, with the bairns round the wash tub she was singing them an old Gaelic washing song, suddenly there was a loud knocking on the back door, drying her hands on her apron as she scurried along the passage. Through the small window in the door she could see the cheese cutter hat worn by the Postal workers of that era. On opening the door she was confronted by the local postman, "Good morning Mistress MacLeod", he greeted her as he held out the dreaded yellow envelope containing a telegram. With her hands shaking she struggled to get it open, the postman stood in silence, she eventually managed and then proceeded to read the contents.

It briefly said that Mhari's bother's-in-law were to report to their nearest Drill Hall immediately, she was overcome with emotion and felt quite weak. Mhari had worked in London in her younger days and had rubbed shoulders with Royalty, she could be deemed as being a right Royalist although in her humble position in the Royal Household she had been a lowly cook, none the less she spoke fondly of members of the Royal family especially Prince Edward who briefly became King in

Nineteen Thirty Six. Anyhow on reading the telegram for the umpteenth time she decided it was an instruction from the King himself and took it upon her self to get hold of the brothers-in-law. She called on her near neighbour Mrs Dougal to ask if she would keep an eye on the bairns while she headed for the hill to alert the ones required to join the war effort as soon as possible. She had a reasonable idea where they would be working, they were preparing the ground for the forth coming autumn deer cull. Mhari was getting exhausted she had been walking for near an hour over very uneven terrain, she was overjoyed when on cresting a small hillock she spied the men about quarter of a mile away. Shouting and waving her arms she managed to attract the attention of the nearest man. It was her brother-in-law Dougal, he came racing along the track to meet her, "What wrong"? Dougal asked, Mhari handed him the little yellow envelope as she tried to regain her breath. Dougal had a quick scan at the contents then started to shout "Hamish, Hamish come here man", Hamish dropped the tools he was using and came running over to where his brother and sister-in-law were standing. Dougal started to speak, "Its from the war office we have to report to the drill hall as soon as possible wearing our T.A uniforms" Hamish being a big gallus guy, was more or less pushing people out of the way saying to his brother, "Come on Dougal lets get at them". He was told just to calm down a minute until the Head keeper arrived, he had been working farther along the hill but had heard the commotion, he was now heading back to where the rest were gathered. The Head Keeper had seen active service in the First World War so his teuchterish looks belied the knowledge he had of what lay beyond Glen Gair, he was known as Buckshot MacLennan the reason for the nickname was he had a great saying, on hearing poachers had been caught he would comment they should be given two barrels of buckshot in the arse that would stop their poaching. Anyhow Buckshot arrived and a plan was hatched the two Macleod brothers would head for home with Mhari, Buckshot would go and speak to the Colonel and maybe persuade him to allow the chauffeur to drive them to the station. He was delighted when the Colonel decided the Chauffer could drive them to Ft William to the drill hall, after and all it was a major emergency. Word soon spread round the village that the

Macleod boys had been called up and before too long another four had received the dreaded telegram, Mhari was fussing about trying to rustle up some food before the boys took off. There was a loud knock on the door, she answered it and got the shock of her life to find the Laird standing on her door step, as was usual in the presence of somebody as important as the Laird Mhari was all bowing and curtseying after and all they were Toffs, she had been trained to respect them. He asked if he could have a word with the two departing employees, she was in a dilemma would she call them out or ask the Laird into her humble residence, her mind was made up when she realised that it was drizzling rain.

The Laird shook hands with the brothers and wished them well, he then told them that the Estate joiner would pick them at two thirty as he had to go to town for ironmongery goods. Bye the time the lads were ready to leave Donald had arrived home, the word had spread round the Glen like wild fire that the Macleod boys had been sent for along with at least four others. Dead on half past two Willie MacLennan the Estate Joiner arrived he had a vehicle that would hold six people along with the driver so he was able to transport the six Glen boys to the Drill Hall in Ft William. Willie MacLennan was a brother of Buckshot the Head Keeper he was also a Veteran of the First World War, he had been wounded early on in the war and was unfit for front line Service, he was drafted into a support Battalion where he learned skills as a Joiner, this held him in good stead when he was demobbed, he was recruited to work for the Laird as estate Handyman. His duties included Joinery, Bricklaying, Masonry and any other type of repairs needed to keep the Estate running, Willie went by the nickname of Willie Chaps, the reason for this was when he was requested to look at a repair job he would weigh up the offending part then turn to who so ever may be with him and say "Ach a couple of chaps wie a claw hammer will put it right", hence the nick name Chaps.

With much hugging and hand shaking the MacLeod brothers left Glen Gair at twenty to three on the fifth of September nineteen thirty nine, the little van was fairly crowded by the time they had picked up the sixth member of the party bound for the unknown, none of the lads had ever been out of Inverness-shire in their lives before, the Macleod's had been in Lewis visiting brother Donald when he worked over there.

The six lads represented a big proportion of the young men of Glen Gair there were the Macleod brothers two Stewart Brothers young Kenny Ross and Hustien Fraser, apart from the Macleod's who were in their late thirties the other four were teenagers. They were all Territorial Army Volunteers and their active service experience amounted to being involved in week-end exercises, they had absolutely no idea what lay ahead of them. Chaps pulled up at the drill hall at just on three thirty, the place was heaving as young men dressed in battle dress were arriving from all over the West Coast, there were queues of them all picking up bits and pieces needed before the could embark to fight the enemy.

Hamish and Dougal joined one of the queues and stated to shuffle along behind the ones in front, Hamish got a bit of a shock when he noted that the clerk seated at the table at the front of his queue was asking questions and filling in forms with the answers, Hamish asked one of the lads who had already signed in what was going on, he near collapsed when the guy told him that the clerk had to confirm that the information they had about you was correct i.e. home address, next-of-kin and date of birth, Hamish went into shock he had given his date of birth as two years younger than he actually was, the age limit was thirty nine he was forty one next birthday he was sure if they twigged he would be sent home, his heart was set on helping defend his country so he decided to brazen it out, he had been born in eighteen ninety eight but to allow him to join the T.A he had said his D.O.B was nineteen hundred. The clerk had his application form in front of him, he asked if there were any changes to the original information, Hamish told him, "Aye my next-of-kin has changed".

"My parents are deceased so its now my bother Donald and his wife Mhari", he was relieved when told that would be all. They stayed the night in Ft William in very temporary accommodation and shipped out next morning to a training depot, of the six Glen Gair men two were sent to the Cameron Highlanders two to the Seaforth Highlanders the other two were sent to the Royal Engineers, it would be a few years before they set foot in Glen Gair again some of them never.

The Macleod house in Glen Gair had a strange feeling about it that night, instead of eight around the dining table their numbers had been reduced to six. When Donald had finished saying grace that evening and every other evening he asked the Lord to keep his brothers and all the young men involved in the war safe. The folks of Glen Gair hardly noticed there was a war going on, they had a few troops passing through, but they kept abreast of what was happening through the daily Newspapers and of course some folks were fortunate enough to have a wireless although the reception could be a bit ropey at times, although there was no visible signs of war the result of the rationing soon began to take affect, but only the essentials like salt and sugar much of which was imported.

The two brothers had been away for nearly four months, it was into a New Year nineteen forty nobody in the Glen had any idea what was going on but rumour had it that the Fifty First Highland Division had been sent to the South of France, this was to re-in force the First and Second Battalions who were Regulars the Fourth and Fifth Battalions were the Territorial Battalions. All that was known of the Glen Gair boys was they had been sent to the Continent. After the evacuation of Dunkirk nothing was heard of them, they either perished or were taken prisoner it would take time to unravel the mess and tell relatives exactly what the situation was. Back in the quiet backwater of Glen Gair life just ambled on, apart from the media reports nothing unusual was happening, the youth's of the Glen reached call up age and were shipped out, but war was just something that was happening miles away.

But the Glen folks were in for a rude awakening when it was discovered that a German Bomber had dropped a bomb on the Cullachy Locks on the Caledonian Canal luckily it never exploded and no damage was done. Then when daylight broke the next day it was discovered that the Aluminium Works at Ft William had also been bombed, again the bombs failed to explode. But the Germans were targeting the Smelter as it produced valuable material needed in the manufacture of aeroplanes this made the powers that be sit up and take notice, with-in weeks an Observer Post was erected near

Laggan Bridge and four local men recruited and trained to man the post round the clock. Donald MacLeod was one Dan Fraser who owned the mail bus, Sandack McConnell and Jonnie McInch who was a veteran of the first world war, ex RFC, he considered himself an expert at plane spotting.

Back in the MacLeod household the rationing was having effects on the standard of food available so Mhari decided to put her Hebridean skills to good use, the skills she had been taught by her mother and father when she was a young girl growing up on Lewis. Firstly she acquired a couple of goats, thus making sure they had a plentiful supply of fresh milk and cheese, she already had a dozen or so hens.

She was also inundated with sic lambs, these lambs were orphans and they needed to be hand reared or put down so Mhari would take them and rear them some times as many as eight or ten. She would fatten them up ready for the spring sales holding on to the best one which she would get butchered, she would cure some of the meat so that none was wasted. Then she would get the gubbins needed to make the Black Pudding (Marak) and White pudding, another part of the ration store was a small wooden barrel in which she would Salt Herring (skatan) or Makerel so they were pretty well self sufficient, of course they were a pretty close knit community so many of the items were shared around. Donald also had a big vegetable patch which he cultivated every year. Both he and Mhari were crack shots, so no rabbit or any edible game was safe to come with-in a hundred yards of the back door. Donald also had a subject very dear to his heart this was his Free Church Relegion he had become involved with the Free Church while working in Lewis, his religion became a big part of his life in as much as he eventually carried out the duties of a Lay Preacher officiating at the church on Sunday, in this capacity he carried out the duties of a fully qualified minister, in later years his services were in big demand and he travelled all over the Highlands preaching the Sunday Sermon where ever they didn't have a full time minister, sometimes relieving ministers who were on holiday. Although he was a deeply religious man he never ever interfered in anybody else's beliefs nor did he go around trying to get people to believe in what he believed in, he was a true christain.

The war was still raging in Europe and almost every corner of the world the young men were being slaughtered wholesale it was a very difficult time and a struggle at times to survive. Apart from the Obsever Post and the odd squad of troops carrying out exercises in the Glen war was something that was happening else where. Then one morning as the men of Glen Gair started to move out to their various work places they were confronted by a squad of Royal Engineers, just opposite the Hotel, they were erecting a barrier across the road. The Forestry Lorry stopped and the driver asked what was going on, the officer in charge told them that they were erecting a barrier and as soon as it was operational they would need to show their Identity Cards before they were allowed to pass through. This new fangled idea caused much disruption, the barrier was to be manned twenty fours a day, if you arrived at the barrier without identification you were not allowed to pass, it was a case of about turn and head home for the all important document, this caused many arguments between military and locals, what annoyed them most was, you maybe only needed to have access for a few minutes, when you returned the soldiers would greet the person by their christian name and then demaned to see their identity card on many occasions it almost came to fisty cuffs. To crown it all if you had forgotten your card all that was needed to be done was to nip down by the river walk along the bank and you could bye pass the offending barrier, it became a game of wits between barrier guards and locals, a wind up situation where the locals would go out of their way to annoy the troops some of whom were none too bright and although they were soldiers all they were fit for was manning remote barriers.

The war was rumbling on still no word from Hamish or Dougal, it was over a year since they had left home. Mhari had contacted the Red Cross to see if they could solve the problem and put their minds at rest. Donald had managed to get a steady job with the Timber Control which was good as he was settled and could map out a routine, he also combined his duties around his voluntary job as an Observer. He had been called up in the First World War but had failed his Medical, now he was too old so he felt he was contributing to the War effort as an Observer. The Glen Gair folks finally received word of the loved ones who had been involved in St Valery and Dunkirk, for the Macleod's the word was not good. Hamish had been taken prisoner along with many other young men from the Great Glen area it was believed they were interned in Poland, the news of Dougal was not so good he was believed to have been Killed in Action near Dunkirk this caused some doom and gloom in the Glen, Dougal was the first son of the Glen to die for his country.

By the middle of nineteen Forty Three Glen Gair was seeing a lot of troop movement, Tanks, Lorries, Dispatch riders all milling about the village, rumour had it that soon the British aided by the Americans were going to invade Europe it was all hush hush stuff and Security in the Glen was tightened up, if they could not prove who they were, or what their business was they were libel to be arrested. Another intriguing chapter of this era was the exercises carried out by the Commandos from near by Locheil, it was rumoured they used live ammunition and people were actually killed but this was never confirmed, of course there was plenty water around Glen Gair where they could carry out all sorts of amphibious manouvers. This carried on well into the spring of nineteen forty four and as suddenly as the troops appeared they disappeared, gone destination unknown at that point in time.

The News for the Macleod family was good and bad, they received a letter from Hamish, it caused quite a stir in the village as it had the Nazi Swastica stamped on it, all that they could gather from the letter was that Hamish was alive and being well treated everything else had been censored and scored out, Hamish being who he was tried adding some information using Galeic words but the Germans took no chances and scored them out as well. Soon after that they received confirmation from the war office that L/Cpl Dougal Macleod had lost his life at Dunkirk. War is a nasty business and soon Mhari received word from Lewis that her only brother John had been called up at the end of nineteen forty three, more worry for her as they were unsure how the war was progressing. The news papers were full of headlines which turned out in many cases to be Propaganda trying to keep the spirits of the nation on a high.

It had all been quiet in the Glen for a few weeks, the new year had arrived and they were now entering the spring of nineteen forty four, they were still receiving censored letters from Hamish and the final confirmation that Dougal had lost his life at Dunkirk, the war was still raging in Europe and the Far East. But communications being what they were in the Forties events were weeks old before the man in the street heard about them. Suddenly the press and the Wireless were full of stories relating to the Invasion of Normandy the horror stories were filtering back causing friends and relatives untold worry. The word was that there were thousands killed or wounded, but the World Leaders of the day were sure that they had done the right thing.

The world had suffered five years of hardship and misery it had to be ended one way or another. Mahri worried about her brother John all she knew about him was that he was a Royal Engineer, his where abouts unknown. It took over a month of hard fighting before the Germans began to give way, there were many deaths on both sides, the legacy of this War and the First one are there for all to see with the amount of Cemeteries and Memorials that litter the French, Dutch and Belgian country side it is a heart breaking sight.

Due to the mayhem of the war, communications were a bit slow so many of the Normandy casulties took weeks to report, of course the relatives back in Britain had very little idea of who had landed in Normandy and who hadn't, out of the blue the dreaded telegram would arrive with the news that a brother, son, husband or maybe a near relative had been wounded or in the extreme killed in action. One such telegram was delivered to a croft in Lewis, Mhari Macleod's sisters had the dreaded word that their only brother John had lost his life as he landed on Sword Beach Normandy, according to his head stone in the British War Cemetery at Bayaux he was killed on the tenth of June nineteen forty four, Mhari was devastated her only brother, how much more sadness were people expected to withstand. Eventually the sacrifises of Normandy began to pay dividends and the Germans were pushed back until they were defeated. Hamish Macleod arrived home in the Spring of nineteen forty five, he was quite malnourished but he had an even bigger problem than that, in as much as his eyesight had been badly damaged due to the forced labour they had to endure working in the Salt Mines in Poland, he would never have full sight again this meant that he was unable to hold down a proper job. But Hamish had a unique situation one of which I never ever fully understood, he was the only man that I ever heard of who was awarded a pension paid for by the German Government it was paid to him every twelve weeks until he died, in the Sixties he was receiving about forty pounds a week, considering that the average wage for a working married man was a take home of around six pounds a week Hamish was well off he spent much of his life living with friends and relations where he indulged in his favourite past time drinking whisky.

As each serving service man or woman arrived home they were welcomed back into the community by the welcome home committee, who arranged a bit of a doo for them. Sadly of the forty six men and women who left the Glen to do their bit for King and Country five never returned, at one time twenty five percent of the population were away from the Glen doing their bit. By the end of nineteen forty five all the fighting of World War Two was over and peace was being enjoyed once again. Most of the men returning to Glen Gair went back to their old jobs mostly employed by the forestry. Col Mellis had to cut back on estate workers as the sporting side of the Estate had taken a hit during the war and the future looked bleak because without the shooting and fishing the income dropped dramatically, eventually the Forestry bought over huge areas of land and left the estates with just enough to survive on. The next big headache for the Estate owners was all the property they owned ie Estate Workers cottages,the Hotel and the shop, they were all in need of upgrading a task that would cost thousands of pounds, money they didn't have. The decision was eventually taken that the property would be sold, the sittting tenants were offered first choice, most of the cottages were sold for around one hundred pounds.

The shop and the hotel were bought for undisclosed sums of money Col Mellis's Empire was shrinking by the day. Of course nineteen forty seven was to herald wholesale changes in as much as the National Health

Service was born. Every British resident was now looked after by the State, everything was free, glasses, teeth and medication, of course human nature being what it is before too long the system was being very badly abused, as the years rolled by the abuse has got worse, even in those early days the older people said one day the well will run dry. How true this statement has turned out to be, 2010/2011 has proved that the extravagant speed at which we live now-a-days has put a huge burden on our country. The very worrying part is that we don't seem to have the people at the top to keep a grip on things, but then most of them would help themselves to the tax payers money if they were sure they wouldn't get caught.

THE KLONDIKE YEARS

Nineteen forty seven saw many changes outwith the new NHS, systems that were needed during the war were no longer required so they were shut down and the men made redundant none more so than the Timber Control run by the Government to make sure that the Coal Mining Industry was supplied with Pit Props and other needs where timber was essential. Donald Macleod found himself without a job his part of the Timber Control was first to go. They were offered work with a private Timber Contractor's who paid very poor rates and at times were very unreliable, the Forestry Commission had vacancies. They had just opened up a huge nursery where they reared their young trees, the employees in the nursery were mainly female.

Donald had a stroke of good luck when he bumped into a neighbour and fellow Glen Gair native. Sandy Taylor because of the dark colour of his skin was known as Alex Dubh in English that means Black Alex, he told Donald that the County Council were looking for men for the road squad. They were opening a depot in Glen Gair, he had already secured the foreman's job, they were getting a lorry and Big Stroopak Mathieson had already secured the post of driver, he was well known as a lazy sort of character who always seemed to land the easiest jobs available, he was given the name Stroopak because of his love of drinking tea, the west coast name for a drink of tea, if you visited the Big Fellow at his home after being welcomed he would ask "Would you have time for a Stroopak". The fourth member of the squad was Sandak McConnell, Sandak had served in the first war and many believed he suffered shell shock, he lived with his younger sister a spinster, only she knew the troubled life Sandak had to endure due to his wartime mental scars. No councilling or medical treatment was offered, or available to the victims of that awful war it was left to the relatives to try and put the pieces back together.

Nineteen forty seven was to be a big year and the start of a huge project that would transform the Scottish Highlands for ever, in some ways it would also ensure that the standard of living for many Highlanders would improve beyond doubt. The North of Scotland Hydro Electricity Board was about to embark on a program of Hydro Projects that would mean highly paid work for many individuals for the next twenty five years. One of the first Scheme's to kick off was Glen Affric. Two huge dams and a Power Station at Fasnakyle, it was deemed to be the biggest Power Station in the world at the time of Construction. There was a huge workmen's camp in the middle of the village of Cannich, it was a village in its own right complete with a huge recreation hall. There was loads of spin off work associated with the Hydro Schemes in the shape of Pylons to carry the power lines to the nearest Power Grid, they were soon to be seen criss crossing the country side, the two companies involved with the Construction of the Pylons were J.L.Eve and Balfour Beatty they were soon employing a large work force between them, at the same time as all this was on going another large project was being constructed at Fannich in Ross-shire so it was busy times. The Highlands alone could not supply the man power required to man up all the on going work, soon droves of men from Ireland and of course Displaced Persons from the aftermath of the war were flocking North in the search of employment.

One story that was circulating at the time was that on one project a Polish guy had managed to get a job as a Foreman he soon sent for fellow Poles to come and work for him, for this act of kindness he charged his Polish Comrades a fee for getting them a job. Back in Glen Gair the younger men were soon hearing about the huge wage packets being paid by the Hydro. They soon gave up their poorly paid jobs with the Estate and the Forestry and joined the ranks of the highly paid hydro men. In reality the reason the wages were better than the Forestry and the Estate was the amount of hours they worked, the Forestry and Estate worked approx a forty five hour week, on the Hydro Schemes the hours would be seventy six minimum, after eight hours they would be paid an enhanced rate of time and a quarter, all day Saturday it was time and a half and on Sunday they would get double time, along with this many sites paid production bonuses so it was easy to double or in some cases treble their wages if they were prepared to concentrate on doing nothing with their lives but work.

The Hydro Schemes attracted quite a lot of undesirable characters, a new word to bandied about was the LDKs, the Long Distance Kids sometimes known as Milestone Inspectors, these were guys who were down and out, drop outs if you like, many had drink problems and in some cases mental health problems. The LDKs would head for the Highlands all Nationalities of them it was referred to as being on the make, in other words they were scroungers some of them would get employment but quite often as soon as they had the first wage they were off on the booze again they soon became well known and nobody would take them on. Most of the companies would run a works bus to Inverness on a Saturday Evening this allowed the workers to let their hair down after a long week of hard work. As soon as the bus pulled up in the town it would be engulfed with LDKs looking for a hand out, the Hydro Men were kind hearted guys who would throw a few shillings at the scroungers. With what ever they managed to obtain they would scurry away to the Chemist and buy the ingredients to make some Surge this consisted of a bottle of Surgical Spirits and one of Orange Squash, when mixed it turned the colour of milk, it was powerful and I would presume that once you were hooked on it your life span would be very short, the price of the two bottles would probably have been in the region of twenty five to thirty pence.

Another two words unheard of in the Highlands before the Hydro Schemes was the Crown and Anchor men, another breed of guys who peddled misery on his fellow man. Crown and Anchor was a gambling game played on a board using dice, the men who owned the apparatus often had difficulty getting into the camps as organised gambling without a proper Government licence was a very serious offence but this maybe added to the thrill or buzz the gamblers achieved, so to gain entry into the camps these guys would have to take a job, usually they went for something not too strenuous such as making tea and keeping the area around the tea shack tidy another part of their duties would be to make up little sand bags used in the tunnels when blasting took place, they were quite happy to spend twelve hours per day just tootering about earning a wage and gambling at every little opportunity they found.

The workmen had to pay for the tea, sugar and milk themselves so every Friday after they had been paid (it was cash in a pay packet then) the tea boy would go round the hut collecting next weeks tea money, usually about half-a-crown (12.5p) each, one well known gambler would offer you the chance to gamble the tea money. On the toss of a coin if you called correctly, heads or tails you either paid nothing or else it cost you double which was five shillings (25p) but the real gambling took place in the camp on a Friday evening usually in the wash room many of the men especially the Irish often lost a whole weeks wages through their own stupidity it was a vicious circle often fights would break out and the police would be called to sort things out .

Eventually one of the well known Crown and Anchor boys was found murdered, it was a rather barbaric killing down near the central belt. The guy involved the Gambler Doherty arrived on one of the huge sites in Argyllshire it was rumoured that he was carrying a large sum of money, that is large for the sixties. Anyhow on the Saturday evening a works bus took a load of workmen into Oban for an evening in the pubs. The driver of the bus had a feeling something was caught round his back axle, on closer examination he discovered a body, it turned out that the body had been stuffed down the inspection hatch over the back axle and had trailed along the road for about thirty miles it was Doherty. Who ever did this awful killing was trying to make the corpse unrecognisable but their evil deed didn't reap any rewards as Doherty had left his brief case with the local Postmistress when the police opened it there was some where between three thousand and eight thousand pounds the exact amount was never confirmed, as far as I am aware nobody was ever caught for that brutal killing. But if you are to get involved in breaking the law especially where money is involved greed often leads to heartbreak.

Back in Glen Gair life was moving on it was getting near the end of the Forties people were starting to recover from the aftermath of the war. All the men and most of the women were working, although married women were full time house wives then. The Forestry was the biggest employer in the North of Scotland and Glen Gair was no exception, there was a Squad of men making access roads throughout the forests, there was a Nursery nearby where they raised seedlings, they were raised until they were big enough to plant, most of the Nursery workers were women, then there was the Squad of men who actually maintained the Forests. To add to this the spin offs from the Forestry were enormous with private Sawmills springing up all over the place, their biggest customer was the Coal Mining Industry most of their mines were propped up using timber, the railway was also one of the big customers as they constantly needed wooden sleepers, timber was a big part of life during the fifties and sixties, in the Highland Glens if not the whole of Scotland.

Life in Glen Gair was lived at a very slow moving pace there were very few motor cars, none of the houses had proper sanitation, nor had they electricity. Survival for the wives and mothers was tough going with every thing done by hand, money was scarce so they had to mend and make do. The bairns were educated as far as the qualifying class (primary five) in the local school, then they were bussed to Ft William to finish their education, a McBraynes Bus with utility seats would pick them up at the back of eight then drop them off at five, the buses were pretty Spartan affairs.

For entertainment most houses had a wireless powered by wet and dry accumulators, there was Badminton once a week in the village hall, a Whist Drive would be held occasionally as were dances on a Friday evening, the ladies of the Glen had the WRI. The men of the Glen probably had the best deal in as much as they had the pub, the wooden shed built away from the main hotel, Capt Blunt, Mien Host didn't want the local serfs mingling with his guests so the only place they were allowed to buy booze was in the shed. The barman was usually a local man who was capable of out drinking many of his customers and often did. Friday and Saturday evening was the favoured drinking evenings but the hours were very curtailed the pub was open from eleven am until three pm then in the evening from five pm until nine pm, nine thirty in the summer. These hours had to be very strictly adhered to. At ten to nine the barman would call last orders, there would be a stampede for the bar,seeing it was last drinks everybody would be needing doubles and possibly a screw top to carryout (a reviver for the morning). Then at dead on nine-o-clock the barman would shout drink up and he would close the hatch. They had ten minutes to clear the bar, quite often the police would appear at eight minutes past, then dead on ten past nine anybody still holding a glass would be ordered to lay it on the counter, if they attempted to have another howf the police would charge them with drinking after hours. During the husbands two or three hours in the pub he would probably demolished about a third of his pay packet, this left the wife with about two thirds on which to keep the house and the husband in what ever kind of tobacco he favoured, bearing in mind the take home pay in the nineteen fifties would be in the regeion of six pounds a week they didn't have much spare cash about.

But since nineteen forty seven things were looking up all medication and visits to the doctor were free and of course every family was given Family Allowance paid for by the State. The first payment was five shillings (25p) for every child after the first so a family of five would receive one pound a week it must have been a godsend. But life was improving all the time with many new products appearing on the market even although some items were still rationed. Then suddenly Glen Gair was invaded by the Pylon Builders, most of them were travelling men and they required accommodation, soon every house in Glen Gair was bursting at the seams as they were filled with as many lodgers as they could cram in, in some cases the locals would turn outhouses into places for the family to sleep so that they could maximise their income from the lodgers, they knew it would be short term so make hay while the sun shone. The boys building the Power Lines were full of stories about a huge new Hydro Scheme to being built in Glen Gair, the locals were very sceptical and the normal comment was that they would believe it when they read it in the Press.

THE HYDRO SCHEME

Then in early nineteen fifty the whole community were invited to attend a meeting in the village hall, the committee who had been elected to carry out the welcome home celebrations at the end of the war had carried on representing the community so they were invited, in their role of ambassadors for the Glen. The hall was packed to capacity as the committee took their places on the stage, there were nine of them but there were seats for eleven. Col Mellis the chairman stood up and addressed the gathered crowd, "Ladies and Gentlemen firstly I would like to welcome you and thank you all for turning out to-night. I am sure by the time the meeting is over you will be able to dispel all the rumours that have been floating around the Glen regarding the Construction of a Hydro Scheme in our midst." He continued "To night we have two men who represent A) the North Of Scotland Hydro Electric Board and B) the Main Contractor responsible for carrying out the work, would you please welcome Mr Ed Morrison and Mr Brian Flanagan". The two men were applauded on to the stage, Flannigan sat down while Morrison spoke, he thanked the Glen people for the support they were showing, then went on to outline what was happening he made his input very brief then handed over to Brian Flanagan. It was noted that Flannigan had a slight trace of an Irish brogue he started to speak, "Ladies and Gentlemen thank you for your support here to-nite, I will try and be as brief as possible but it is important that we cover all aspects of this huge project, there will undoubtedly be points we may not agree upon but we can note them and come back and iron them out at a later date." "I represent the Main Contractor Powermax, we have many years of experience in the Construction Industry, one of our main concerns in any area we work in is, that we get along with and keep the local people happy which we aim to do here". "We hope to start work within six weeks, at the moment we are negotiating with your Chairman Col Mellis the purchase of Craigend Lodge where we intend housing our Engineers and Senior Foremen. Just across the road on the flat field between the Lodge and the river we intend erecting the workmen's accommodation with enough room to house three hundred and fifty men, we will have a Police Station with a full time police man, a Cinema to which all the local people are invited to use if they feel inclined and we have a wet canteen where the men can purchase beer if they feel the need of a refreshment." The audience was silent as they listened to what was being said, Flanagan continued, "We will be running an apprenticeship scheme for any of your young folks interested in obtaining a trade, we will train Joiners, Electricians and Plant Fitters, there may even be opportunities for Trainee Engineers. Flanagan had talked none stop for nearly an hour, it was decided to have a fifteen minute break as most people smoked and were probably gasping.

During the break one or two small groups of Glen folks had got together and were deciding on what questions could be asked, they may never get the chance again, on the agenda was a question and answer section. Flanagan spent most of his working time in a big busy office just outside London so he was well pleased with himself to get out into the sticks and find out how the other half live, he was delighted with proceedings so far.

He was quite convinced he had the Hill Billies eating out of his hand, the meeting would be wound up with-in an hour and he would be heading back to Inverness in good time. He was booked in the Kingsmills Hotel one of the finer establishments in the Highland Capital. The meeting was called to order by Col Mellis, Mr Flannagen was invited to conduct the question and answer shedule, quite a few of the locals asked various questions relating to how the work would proceed. The first man to ask a question was Stroopak his was quite simple "How many hours a week would the site be working"? Flannagen stood up and gave a spiel about the tight schedule, his company had to complete the Contract in five years, clearing his throat he continued, "In view of our shedule and the fact we will be asked to pay hefty compensation if the contract runs over, it is necessary for us to work round the clock seven days a week," he did not anticipate the uproar this statement would cause but it came to a near riot. Donald Macleod normally a very placid man was on his feet waving his arms about and shouting, "There will be no seven day working in this Glen we obseve the Lords day very strictly and we have never allowed work to take place on the Sabbath ever" all around Duncan his fellow church goers could be heard muttering "here here" Flanagan was struck dumb the Hill Billies had a voice, at last they found an item that didn't please them. He hummed and hawed for a few minutes then turned to the person taking notes and asked for this to be recorded, that the working week was a point of contention which would have to be persued at an other extra ordinary meeting. An hour and a half later the meeting wound up the Glen folks had managed to screw a few bits and pieces out of the company for example they agreed to fund the kids Christmas Party during their stay in the Glen. A question was asked about any of the men being caught poaching the river, the water Baliff Jock McGhee a bit of a stickler for making sure law and order was kept on his beat on the river requested assurance that any of the men working for Powermax caught poaching would be dismissed by the company, and that this threat should be displayed around the camp to make sure they were all aware of the rules. Flannagen agreed to this request and assured his audience that any worker stepping out of line in an unjust manner would be instantly dismissed. The issue of the working week would be looked at in ten days time when Flanagan would be back in the Glen it was decided that all three churches would be represented at the meeting along with the rest of the committee members.

The Locals or Hill Billies as Brian Flanagan liked to refer to them, had soon christened him as the Soot (suit) in the Gaelic it sounded like Zoot, he was given this name as he was always dressed immaculately in a Saville Row suit, and quite often he had a change daily, pointing to the fact that he was never at the rock face. Stroopak referred to him as the Company hatchet man his main job was making the serfs toe the line. The three main Church Leaders had had numerous get-to-gethers over the next ten days, for once in their lives they were showing signs of Solidarity in their opposition to working on the Sabbath. The meeting which was put on hold ten days ago was resumed in a class room in the School as there was only going to be eight or nine people attending no need to open the village hall with the expence of heating, lighting and they would have to pay the care taker to make sure the Tilley lamps were kept going.

Brian Flanagan was invited to kick off the meeting after the attendees were welcomed by the Chairman Col Mellis. Flanagan cleared his throat and started to speak, "Gentlemen my fellow directors and I, of Powermax, have had a busy ten days trying to thrash out a solution to our difference of opinion regarding the working week proposed by our Company." "Normally we would work from seven-o-clock on Sunday Morning through to four-o-clock on Saturday afternoon, overnight on Saturday we would carry out maintinance, this means we would have men working seven days a week. But in view of the Glen Gair inhabitants being against working on the Sunday we have compromised and we will close down Saturday afternoon as usual and resume production work at seven pm on Sunday evening" he looked around the assembled crowd for a reaction and was quite taken aback when all he saw was shaking heads. After a moment of complete silence the Zoot started to speak, "Gentlemen I am putting the ball back in your court by asking what is acceptable to you"?. Donald MacLeod was on his feet, this was his bone of contention, he was not prepared to move one inch, "Meester Flannagan your question is easily answered no work on the Sabbath Day which starts at midnight on Saturday and ends at midnight on Sunday that is all we ask", the Church of Scotland Minister was nodding in agreement. Flannagan asked that the meeting be adjourned until he had further discussions with his head quarters, he asked if they could re-convene in two hours time it would be getting on for ten pm before they got back together. Flanagan was getting a bit frustrated the Hill Billies were starting to get up his nose, normally the company just moved in and started work but seeing this was a huge contract the company had decided to give the locals a say on how they would go about their business, he did not envisage that Religion would play such a big role in the way things were shaping up. He had booked a room in the Local Hotel where he had access to a telephone his fellow board members were waiting for his call and they were none too pleased when they found out his news was a negative, they bandied the problem about for a while, the question was asked did he think the Hill Billes were looking for a bung (back hander), no Brian Flannagan thought they were far too honest to be trying any under hand tactics. About an hour later London and Flannagan had come up with a plan where they would suggest that they would prospone production working until seven pm on the Sunday that was a whole twelve hour change to their normal work pattern, but they would still use the time to carry out essential mentinance. When Flannagan had left the class room Donald Macleod had nipped home, when he got there Alex Dubh (Black Sandy) was sitting chatting to Mhari over a cup of tea, he asked Donald how the meeting had gone, Donald told him it was stale—mate and they were continuing in about an hour. Donald continued and relayed all that had been said at the meeting and stressed that he would not agree to any work taking place in Glen Gair for the twenty four hours of the Sabbath unless it was a life or death emergency. Alex lit his pipe and through the haze of black twist smoke which both he and Donald were belching out he asked a question, "Tonald are you aware that when they set off a blast in the Tunnel that there are eight to ten bangs" Donald looked at his workmate and shook his head.

"No Alex indeed I didn't know that, how does that come about?" "Well I was talking to my cousin over in Glen Affric you know Hamish the Keeper he was telling me its not one bang but like a machine gun going off and lasts for about ten seconds but he had no idea why that was." Alex Dubh was known by this name because of the mop of black curly hair he had, it gave him more of a Spanish appearance than a Glen Gair man but Alex had been born and bred in the Glen, he had failed to join the Army in nineteen eighteen because of his poor eyesight which required him to wear thick Jellie Jar type glasses, but Alex was a pretty smart fellow and could talk on many subjects which he had learned about from his great love of reading. His information about the blasting was more fuel for Donald in his quest to stop them working on the Sabbath day, Alex went on to tell him that it annoyed the animals in the Glen as the Cattle, Sheep and Deer would stampede when the blasts went off and that could be as many as eight or ten times a day. Donald pondered for a few seconds and spoke, "Aye Sandy this is what we're up against can you imagine the Sabbath and them blasting away good style we wouldn't get a minute's peace we must stand against it at all costs," Sandy fully agreed even although he wasn't a regular church goer.

Donald was back in his seat and discussing the latest price rises when the door opened and Flannagen re-appeared he apologised for the delay but explained how difficult it was to raise any of his fellow directors. He didn't take a seat but stood with his back to the blackboard and started to tell of the latest plan they had come up with to try and apease the local worshippers. "Gentlemen I have just spent an hour with my fellow directors thrashing out a work policy that we hope will be to your liking". "We will work our normal week Monday to Friday i.e. two twelve hour shifts, on Saturday our last shift will finish at four pm. On the Sunday we will start production work at seven pm", he looked around the room grinning as though he had just won the pools, but nobody else cracked a light, the Zoot continued, "are we all happy with that arrangement"?. He could feel a sinking feeling in the pit of his stomach as he surveyed the room and noted that all the heads were shaking form side to side, in normal circumstances he would have blown his top and told them that was it take it or leave it, but he had a delicate situation on his hands and if it went to court it could be costly, further more the delay could be disastrous. So he had to change tactics, "Gentlemen we are talking about holding up a huge contract being paid for by you people through your taxes, we have gone as far as we are prepared to go, but before we end in stalemate I will put the ball back in your court once again, what ever you suggest we will try and work along that lines" Flannagan needed a stiff drink it was getting near eleven pm, he asked them if they would ajourn until to-morrow night at seven pm. This was agreed, the locals would have a proposition ready for that time, they decided to meet at six thirty and discuss what they wanted. At dead on six thirty the meeting was reconvened, Donald Macleod had an idea that he put before the assembled villagers, what if they agreed to let Powermax commence their operation at nine pm on the Sunday evening with the priviso that there would be no blasting before midnight, that would give them time to have the first blast of their working week a few hours later than they proposed.

He asked for a show of hands, the response was unanimous. Flannagan was due to appear in about ten minutes. Donald Macleod had more or less taken over the role of spokesman so when Flannagan appeared the Laird welcomed him and handed the floor over to Donald. He stood up and cleared his throat before acknowledging Flannagan's presence, "Well Meester Flannagan we have spent a lot of time and thought. Trying to resolve our differences, we have come up with an idea that hopefully will be acceptable to all parties concerned. We have already reluctantly agreed that you can carry out essential maintinence on Saturday and throughout the Sabbath, the bone of contention is the production work, especially the noise from blasting, so we are going along the lines that you will not start production work before nine pm on Sunday evening and that no blasting takes place prior to midnight, what are your thoughts on that Meester Flannagan"?. Fannagan sat for a moment or two drumming the end of his pencil on the desk in front of him. He stood up cleared his throat and spoke "Gentlemen, I on behalf of my company would like to thank you for your understanding and co-operation in trying to resolve this matter. As I have a board of Directors who have to agree all such matters I will need to duscuss with them your generous proposals before we finally put this to bed, so we will close this meeting as of now and I will return early next week for a final summing up of the situation." Donald Macleod held up his hand and asked, "When you return Meester Flanagan we take it if all parties have agreed you will have a written statement showing what we have all agreed, this should be signed by your companies representative and our Chairman". Flannagan stood up and asked was this document really necessary, he pointed out that normally his word was his bond. Donald Macleod argued back that should he Flannagan leave the company for any reason his successor was libel to change the whole proposal and they would be back to square one. The Zoot wasn't winning many points in this argument and the Hill Billies had just scored another when he agreed to draw up a document outlining the working hours, with that the meeting was adjourned until further notice.

The Laird received a phone call from Flannagan to let them know he and his fellow Directors had agreed to meet the conditions demanded by the Glen Folks he would be back in Glen Gair on the Wednesday, could they arrange a meeting in the Village Hall as he wanted to let the Glen folks see what work would be taking place this would be in conjunction with Ed Morrison of the N.S.H.B, he outlined the format of the meeting, stating they would hold a question and answer session, strongly advising that anybody with any queries should have them ready as they may not get another opportunity.

The village hall was bursting at the seems as the Glen Gair folks piled in, all determined to find out what was going to happen to their beloved Glen. Once everyone was settled the Community Committee accompanied by Brian Flannagan, Ed Morrison and A.N.Other filed on to the stage. Col Mellis the chairman started to speak. He welcomed the guests and introduced the third member of the party as Bob Smith the Chief Construction Engineer with N.S.H.B,the Col then handed the platform over to Ed Morrison who thanked everyone for turning out, also for their patience and understanding in clearing up the problem of the seven day working.

He went on to outline the agenda of the meeting. We the panel have brought along a model of where the work sites will be and the work that will take place at each site. Once we have run through it, you can get up from your seats and have a browse then we will have an hour of questions and answers. First on the platform to speak was Bob Smith, there were five different models plus one of the work camp which was now under construction. He cleared his throat and started to speak, "Ladies and gentlemen this is a huge project costing five million pounds it has to be completed and producing electricity with—in five years, Number One site is the Dam across the end of Loch Gair, as soon as we have the camp up and running we will start the Dam in earnest this means a lot of excavations, wooden shuttering, steel and concrete, Number two site is the Fish Hatchery on the out skirts of the Village again there will be a lot of shuttering and concrete,Number three site is the power Station we have to blast a cavern big enough to house the generators so the station will be partially under ground. We require a decent number of stone masons to do the stone work for the power house alone, this will be built from local stone in an attempt to blend it in with the surrounding rock". "Number four site is the surge shaft this is quite an under taking as the shaft is close to one thousand feet deep, number five site is the main Tunnel this carries the water from the Dam to the power station, it is twelve feet by twelve feet and runs for nearly four miles and of course last but by no means least is the workers accommodation, this will house between three hundred and fifty and four hundred men, we have our own Police Station, Medical Room, Shop and a Cinema which will operate three nights per week, any local person wishing to have a night at the pictures will be most welcome. The rest of the panel were asked for any comments but they declined and the meeting was closed for half an hour to let the people have a wander around the models. Just on eight-o-clock the meeting was re-convened Brian Flanagan who had been quiet up until then stood up and asked if there were any questions, quite a few hands were raised and some quite easily answered questions were asked it was nearing eight thirty Flanagan looked at his watch and decided he would allow them another ten minutes then wrap the meeting up at quarter to nine. He was not aware that Alex Duhb had not asked a question yet but he was about to, Alex held his hand up and Flanagan asked what his question was, "Well Meester Flanagan I have listened to all the banter that has gone on about this and that but nobody has questioned you about the Tunneling, I am led to believe that when you detonate a blast in the Tunnel there are about eight bangs instead of just one, and another question on the same subject how many blasts will we have to put up with each day?," hastily adding "that is discounting Sunday". Flanagan was thrown a bit Tunnelling was not his subject, further more the closing time of quarter to nine was receding fast, he turned to the panel and asked the Engineer Bob Smith if he could answer this question. Bob Smith was a quiet man but very knowledgable about his job he had a big responsibility overseeing this contract but he was well aware of every function that would take place.

He began, "Ladies and Gentlemen I will try and explain the answers you are seeking as quickly as possible". He turned to the blackboard and drew a semi circle in the shape of a horse shoe.

"This is the outline of the Tunnel it is twelve feet high and twelve feet wide, before we start tunnelling we need to clear away all the dirt and rubble until we hit hard rock". "We already know the line we are to take so when ever the rock is solid enough we will begin going under ground, the engineers will mark the outline of the tunnel for the first twenty feet then the foremen do it themselves using candle pots suspended from the roof." "The Shift Boss is responsible for the drilling of the rock face he has a pattern to work to so he marks off the position of each hole". "Our tunnel is twelve feet by twelve feet in size and four miles long, so it will require about twenty four holes to be drilled before every blast can be executed. Three holes are drilled in close proximity in the dead centre this set of holes are called the "Cut" only the top and bottom holes are charged with explosives the centre hole is left empty to allow for expansion if this did not happen most likely the explosives would shoot out of the holes because there was no where for the pressure to go. The next set of holes were known as the box, four holes surrounding the cut the next set is the inner ring then the outer ring which includes the crown hole at top dead center the five holes along the floor of the tunnel are known as the lifters there purpose is to loosen up the floor so that the miners can dig a track to lay the narrow gauge railway line on which all the transport runs, a set of rails would be required every twenty four hours. So there you are folks a run down on how a tunnel is driven, after all the holes are drilled they are charged with explosives each hole has one stick of gelignite pushed in as far it will go this explosive has the detonator inserted and the two wires reach out the full eight feet the length of the hole, after each hole has been charged the wires are connected together to form an electrical circuit, to make sure the circuit is sound the wires are tested using an ohmmeter if the reading is good the two wires are then tied to a set of leads and everybody travels back to where there is a battery the lead wires are connected to the battery, the warning signal is given then the button on the battery is pressed to trigger the explosion". "The squad then retire back the tunnel a bit for a much needed tea break or lunch whatever time of day it may be". Bob Smith was starting to get signals from his fellow panel members to speed it up, it was nearing ten-o-clock and they were getting fed up. He briefly told the audience about the Surge Shaft a huge under taking about nine hundred feet deep and thirty feet in diameter, to try and bring the meeting to a close Bob told them the shaft was similar to the tunnel except that it was vertical instead of horizontal. They were sure they had covered everything so the inevitable was asked "Before we close any more questions there was a pause, the Panel were on their feet about to thank the audience for attending, but they hadn't reconed on Alex Dubh. Alex was a native of the Glen a very slow methodical man, he was also a wealth of knowledge even although his education had been pretty basic. Alex was standing with his hand in the air, Ed Morrison was the first panel member to notice him and he couldn't ignore him. The panel stopped moving to-wards the door and asked Alex if he needed further answers. With his best teauchter accent he started to talk, "At one of the previous meetings I asked a question about the blasting in the tunnel and it was neffer properly answered", the rest of the audience could be heard muttering under their breath "We'll be here for a week if they allow the Black Fellow to continue".

Ed Morrison asked what the question was, hastily adding it had slipped his memory. "Well its like this Meester Morrison my question was, why when they blast in the Tunnel there are seven or eight bangs instead of just the one".? Ed Morrison again passed this technical question on to Bob Smith, he cleared his throat and started to speak everybody was seated again hoping it wouldn't take too long. "Well if you think back to the patteren we drill the tunnel face starting with the cut etc, we then charge the face with explosives using what we call delay detonators, this can be from zero to fifteen seconds the idea is". "If all the detonators went off at the one time and one or two on the outer ring were maybe slightly ahead of the inner rings the blast would possibly be aborted this would cause severe problems when we went to drill the rock face again with the possibility of live detonators till buried in the rock, if a drill was to hit them they would exploded causing serious injuries or even death (it has been known to happen)". "So to avoid this situation we use delay detonators starting in the centre of the cut rememeber the three holes in the dead centre, we charge the top and bottom using a number zero leaving the middle hole empty for expansion purposes, we then charge the four holes known as the box using a number two and so on until we only have the crown hole and the lifters which we charge using a number higher than the rest ie five or maybe six, hence the reason instead of hearing boom once you will hear boom boom boom until all the detonators explode." Alex Dubh was asked if he was satisfied with that answer to which he nodded his head, the audience were already moving to-wards the door shaking their heads and looking at the watches which showed it was close to eleven-o-clock. But on the whole they were pleased at what had been achieved along with the no blasting on the Sabbath, Powermax also confirmed that they would sponsor the kiddies Christmas Party for the next six years so all in all it was worth the late night, the Company were also delighted that they were free to carry on working with no further interruptions or hassle.

THE POST WAR GLEN

The war was now almost forgotten, except that is for families who had lost relatives, the younger generations had new found activities to be getting on with. The village hall was a well used facility with events taking place most nights, a youth club, badminton club, WRI and once a month a travelling cinema, also on a regular basis there would be a Friday night dance so all in all there was plenty to take up idle time. The coming of the Hydro Scheme on their door step would no doubt generate further activities as the population in the village would be trebled with-in a matter of months. The works camp site was already a hive of activity with joiners, plumbers, electricians, crane drivers and labourers working flat out to get the place habitable. The first opportunity for locals to enhance their work skills was announced when Powermax employed tradesmen's mates this was more or less an apprenticeship, the school-leavers of that year were the first to benefit from the Scheme. The next leap forward was when it was announced that the Council were to erect sixteen Council Houses, they were badly needed and would come with electricity and bathrooms, virtually the first in the Glen, the few men eligible and available to work on the scheme would hardly scratch the surface of the work force required once production was at full capacity. The older middle aged guys stuck with their regular jobs in the Forestry and the Council and of course the Estate still employed a few Gillies and Stalkers, the Hydro Board the new owners of the River were responsible for employing Water Bailiffs, there was full employment, nobody needed to be idle. Glen Gair was a hive of activity, the roads were teeming with all sorts of vehicles causing wide spread disruption, basically because all roads after you left the main thoroughfare were single track with passing places. Furthermore as well as the Scheme near the mouth of the river Phase one at Loch Huich was also gearing up to start, this was thirty miles further up the Glen in a pretty isolated environment where every last piece of equipment had to make the tedious thirty mile journey on the single track road, a low loader drivers nightmare. The lay-byes were not built for Low Loaders, they were quite short and often had soft verges, the inexperienced driver didn't have his sorrows to seek, there was wonderful scenery but woe betide any driver who dwelt too long on the heather clad mountains, as often as not he would find himself bogged to the axles with no help near at hand.

As soon as there was accommodation available at the work camps there would be workers starting to drift towards Glen Gair. The ones sent by the Dole Office were lucky, if they had been signed on the chances are they would get a warrant to pay their fares if not is would be Shanks's Pony, it was not all plain sailing after walking many miles a chap would arrive on site and there would be no vacancies in this case he had two options carry on up the Glen to Loch Huich or about turn and retrace his steps.

Before the complete project was up and running it had taken about six months erecting the camp and preparing the various work sites. Lots of Peat and loose earth had to be moved to allow access to the hard rock so that tunnelling, the surge shaft and of course the Dam, could commence.

While this was ongoing the manual workers were not required but they were gearing up and recruiting men experienced in the various functions that would be taking place throughout the project duration.

BOG ARABS AND GULLS

The Hydro Schemes were constructed by some real strange characters, odd bodes to say the least, many of them were Industrial Gypsies moving from site to site picking up jobs where ever they could, they were a hardy breed of men who looked after each other. You had to be hardy to stand up to the conditions, i.e. the weather, unless you were a Tunnel Tiger where you were underground but would face different hazards, dust, wet and fumes. One such character was Willie Barron, Willie belonged to Lochaber and went by the nom-de-plume of (Lochy) he was well known on the big construction sites where he had worked since he left school at fourteen. His first job was making tea for the Tunnel Tigers who worked on the huge tunnel associated with the Aluminium Works at Fort William, the year was nineteen twenty two. Since then he had moved around, just before the outbreak of the Second World War he was working in the huge under ground fuel storage depot at Invergordon. Although only in his mid forties Lochy was not a healthy man, this was due to working underground in the most unhealthy conditions, also his fondness of the demon drink. He was unable to work under ground any longer so had to revert back to where he started, making tea for the young bucks who now controlled the under ground workings, he warned many of them to get out before they ended up like him, as he put it "buggered and am nae fifty yet." He had landed his latest job making tea for the tradesmen who were erecting the camp but he preferred working with the tunnel men the tradesmen were too fussy, not like the Tigers who were as rough as a badgers arse. The only complaint the Tigers ever had was that the tea was never sweet enough, they would badger Lochy to add more sugar but he would argue there was plenty sugar in the bucket, it was just that they didn't make it as sweet as they did before the war, the truth was that the fly old Lochy would pocket a bit of the tea money to finance his drink habit. The company paid his wages and supplied accommodation where they could sit and have their break, but the men had to pay for the rations themselves, Lochy used to collect half-a-crown per man that was (12.5p) per week from twenty men, that was two pounds and ten shillings £2.50p he would pocket the fifty pence right away then stretch the two pounds to buy the cheapest rations he could find hence the shortage of sugar. Although only in his mid forties his health was destroyed, due to working too many years under ground breathing in dust and fumes, and of course his constant love affair with the booze although he was always at his work and he could be depended upon. Lochy's week amounted to at most six and a half days working, the other half would find him in oblivion pissed out of his mind, if he ran short of money the ration Kitty was fair game, another reason for the lack of sugar. But for all that Lochy was a popular guy full of stories about by gone days, the younger lads would sit fascinated by some of his exploits. All that was needed to trigger off one of his stories was for a younger guy to moan about the work. "Yea dinna ken what work is, in the big Tunnel at the Aluminium Works most of the guys smoked pipes, the foremen wouldn't allow them time to fill the pipe during working hours so they carried two with them, they filled them at the tea break.

There was no fancy machines to load the muck from the rock face there, they laid big steel plates on the floor of the tunnel and blasted on top of them, then the men loaded the skips using shovels, that lads was what hard work amounted to.

During one conversation some body remarked that the camp was due to open in two weeks time. This was the cue for Lochy to start another of his rants, "Aye yea can look oot then, the place will be hotchin wie Bog Arabs and Gulls", for some of the younger guys this was their first Construction Site, they had served their time in the town and now they were trying to make a quick buck, they were unfamiliar with the Hydro Lingo, so somebody asked "What the bloody hell are Bog Arabs and Gulls", Lochy looked horrified, Bog Arabs are the Irish they will be desperate to get in the Tunnels so that they can earn some cash to send back to the folks in the bog. You'll easy ken when they arrive wearing a fancy suit and wellie boots, that will be them until the first holiday when they'll buy a new suit and head home for the holiday, when they get back to work they go straight into the tunnel wearing the new suit, they hardly leave the camp between holiday breaks." Lochy let out a big sigh and continued, "The Gulls are the Banff-shire men they'll be here for the concrete work, great workers, a lot of them are ex—trawler men and they can work for thirty six hours at a time without sleep probably due to there irregular sleep pattern at sea." "Aye they all have the same deformity deep pockets and short arms every penny's a prisoner and anything they get for nothing is a bonus, one man I kent kept a tin of syrup in his locker, before he spread it on his piece he would sit it on the hot stove for ten minutes until it was like water, then he was unable to spread a thick layer on the bread, speak about being tight."

Another worthy of that era was Humpy Danny Macdonald, Danny had nothing going for him, about five feet four inches tall with a grotesque hump on his back he also stuttered when he spoke. He had been around the Construction Circuit for many years. Unfit for Army service he had worked on many of the war time projects, a native of Ross-shire he was usually employed as a banksman, his favourite crane driver was a fellow Danny Macdonald, they had worked together for years. Humpy Danny,s favourite tale was that on one of the sites they worked on there were thirteen Danny Macdonalds employed there at the one time, he would stutter his way through the story, "Wh, Wh, When wi, wi, we were at ggg Glen Affric th,th,th there wis thirteen Danny Macdonalds on site at the same time". He would then proceed to rhyme them off, "Th,Th,Th, there wis masel Hu, Hu, Hu, Humpy Danny, Danny the crane driver, Mad Donnie the Barraman, Donnie the moonman frae Ballahulish, DDDanny the charge hand joiner and so on until he had named all thirteen. These were just two of the many characters who did their bit to keep the Construction Sites going, as we proceed more will pop up. Lochy was getting up tight about the camp opening he would be moving in, to get away from that moanin bitch of a wife of his, every time she smelt a whiff of drink off him she would start. In the camp he had a permanent supply of screw tops in his locker. He was also anxious to hear from his pal Alex Cameron(Locheil) another Lochaber man, Alex had been a Tunnel Tiger for years at the moment he was working in the London Underground in the compressed air Tunnels but he had his name on the list for Glen Gair his normal job was shift boss, Lochy new that if Lochiel was in charge he would be well looked after.

Shortly after that it was announced that the camp builders were to be disbanded and shifted to different sites such as the shuttering compound where the joiners and their mates would be employed, other trades men plumbers etc went to the Black Gang the name given to the maintenance men.

Lochy was busy tidying his tea shack when there was a feeble knock on the door he looked up and saw one of the young labourers. "Excuse me Lochy I was wondering if I could pick your brains". Lochy was taken aback, it was not often that was he asked to allow somebody to pick his brains, "Aye nae bother ma loon but it'll nae tak lang because if I had brains I widna be here". The young fellow explained that he would like a job where he could learn a trade or some thing like that, his question was how would he go aboot it. Lochy stood back and squinted at the lad "Weel ma loon its nae easy to get into most places in this line of work, yea see to get into the Black Gang yea need tae have the funny hand shake, he tapped the side of his nose and in a lowered voice he whispered Free Masons". "Then there's the Tunnels yea need tae kick we yir left fit, mostly Irish Catholics frae Donegal". "The Seagulls dinna show their allegiance to anybody but themselves, here for the money but if there's trouble they stick the gither like shite sticks tae a blanket." "But if my mate Lochiel gets a shift boss's job I can hae a word wie him and maybe get you the handyman's job on our shift nothing tae it just keep the tunnel face going and you've cracked it, just leave it wie Lochy". As word spread that the camp was about to open droves of men started to turn up at the site labour office, they came by bus,car, motorcycle and on foot. For some it was just a case of leaving their name at the Labour office as the work hadn't started properly, still a lot of preperation to be carried out. It wasn't hard to pick out the Tunnel Tigers all you needed to do was look at the face, the gray coloured skin and sallow complextion was a sure give away, the reason for this was that the tunnel men never really worked in daylight and sunshine, mostly they worked a twelve hour shift, they changed over at the rock face so the shift going off would have been there at least twelve and a half hours, for about half the year they went to work in the dark and went home in the dark hence the awful colour of the skin a very unhealthy means of earning your living, along with the lack of sunshine they had to breathe in damp air and occasionally dust if some eejit decided to drill holes without using water, along with all this hazzards there was the three maybe four ounces of Golden Virginia or Old Holburn that most of the Tigers smoked every week. But all they had to do to see what the future held was to have a look at Lochy and they would see what years of Tunnelling, Smoking and heavy drinking did for their health.

Bye the middle of nineteen fifty the Glen Gair Scheme was going full blast the camp was near full to capacity the only site not fully manned was the surge shaft, a special breed of men worked the shafts mostly Eastern Europeans it was a dangerous hazardous job, once the pilot hole was drilled and open there was a drop of a thousand feet before you hit solid ground, if you fell your chances of survival were nil. The guy in charge at Glen Gair was a right little Hitler and it was rumoured that he was maybe emulating his former leader as he was thought to be an ex SS man, nobody had ever heard of him before but he was Eastern European possibly Cech, Polish or Ukranian, he gave nothing away about his past, the suspicious part was that he had changed his name to McGregor yes Stanislav McGregor.

JUST DESSERT'S

McGregor had a very small team of men, they were still working on the pilot shaft, his squad amounted to half a dozen men all of similar nationality to himself the story was that this guy had a price on his head and that his men were bodyguards. He supposedly had a history of violence, the way he ordered people about was disgusting, as there was no protection such as industrial tribunals in those far off days this guy fired people at will, look at him the wrong way and you were history, the men moaned about him but could do nothing. He pushed his squad to the limits, he got results so Powermax were quite happy to employ the animal. He was pushing hard to complete the pilot shaft it was hoped that in six weeks time the main shaft would commence The idea was, the pilot shaft was a six foot diameter verical tunnel it was driven from bottom to the top, when completed you had a six foot hole about a thousand feet deep. Once this was complete they would start at the top and work their way to the botton the hole would be widened to possibly thirty feet diameter, it was dangerous hazardous work with frequent accidents.

Donald Campbell was a drunken West Coaster who had ruined not only his life but a budding career as an Accountant, due to Donald's love of the whisky bottle and his sticky fingers, he was hounded out of his profession in his early fifties but he had found sanctuary as a Labour Officer/Time keeper on the Construction Sites, his years of being stuck in dingy, dusty little offices the booze and fags had taken its toll and Donald looked to be in worse condition than an ageing Tunnel Tiger.

He hated this McGregor the Pole as he called him, Donald thought he was the most ignorant little man he had ever come across, he was fed up sending men up to his site only for them to be rejected, in fact he started to warn the lads as he recruited them that their time may be limited, but McGregor was on a recruiting drive as he needed more men to work on the shaft so Donald did his best to give him the pick of what was available. Donald was running out of experienced shaft men, he was at the end of his tether when suddenly two well built guys probably mid twenties appeared at the little hatch he opened to talk to the men. Donald asked what he could do for them, as soon as he heard them speak he knew they were Eastern Europeans possibly Polish. The taller of the two spoke in reasonable English "We are lookink for vork" Donald asked, "Have you shaft experience"? both nodded and said "Yah Yah ve haff" Donald was delighted, he then told them about the arsehole they would be working for, if he approved of them. He phoned the shaft office and spoke to MacGregor telling him he had a couple of countrymen of his own claiming they had shaft experience. MacGregor said to hold them there and he would come and have a look at them.

The two Polish lads were married to Scots girls and lived in Ross-shire they had worked at Fannich and in Perthshire before they ended up in Glen Affric doing mostly shaft work when it was available, this hazardous type of work paid the best money. The guys were Stefan and Jan, to their friends and neighbours they were Stevie and Yannie both twenty eight years old and both from the same farming community just outside Krakow in Poland they had a story to tell that would have been a best seller.

The two of them and another friend Josef had been born within hours of each other had gone to school together, they were inseperable, they worked in their farming community helping their fathers, they were very poor people and making ends meet was a struggle.

Suddenly in the first week of September nineteen thirty nine Germany invaded Poland and over ran the place with in days, the three lads then sixteen years old were taken prisoner, the community was torched and burned to the ground, what happened to the other residents was anybody's guess the Nazis were only interested in able bodied men.

Before too long the lads found themselves in a slave labour Battalion just behind the German front line, their task was to construct gun emplacements often blasting out the rock before concrete was used to form the shield,it was hard work often done with very crude tools. They were barely given enough food to survive on, the guards mostly Ukrainian and Latvian were cruel evil men to whom life meant very little, some of the weaker men were just exterminated and often left lying where they were gunned down it was dreadful. The three friends stuck together and looked after each other as best as they could often risking their lives as they stole extra food in their quest for survival. They had survived for three years although very thin and quite weak they were alive, unlike many of their fellow country men who had been murdered some times just to satisfy somebody's bad temper. One morning they were roused early and told to pack their belongings they were moving, they formed up outside their quarters and were marched about three miles to a railway station where they were loaded onto trucks, just crammed in like sardines no food just a bucket of water and one to use as a toilet, conditions were hellish. Thirty hours later the train pulled up, the men were unloaded no idea where they were until one of the railway workers spoke briefly to one of the Polish lads, by the sound of this man they were in France. It turned out that they were in a place called Wizernes five kilometers from St-Omer France at La Coupole, it was the rocket launching site for the V2 rocket, a huge project. The working and living conditions were atrocious and the Latvian Gaurds were the most brutal human beings the lads ever encountered, any man who was unfit for work was shot, if one man fell by the wayside and his friends tried to help they were shot, the sad part was that the dead bodies would lie on the site until the end of the shift then their workmates would be orderd to throw them onto a skip for removal to the surface, they were never seen again it was envisaged that they were dumped over the tip end and buried under the rubble, the lads had never witnessed such brutality before.

The three mates had managed to avoid trouble but it was always just round the corner and the guards were always ready to dish out a beating if the workers stepped out of line. All of a sudden the routine was disrupted, Josef was moved to another part of the site, still underground but in a different area, he found himself along with lads from their home village so he was accepted and fitted into their small gang, their foreman was an army corporal, he was Latvian a proper pig of a man who thought nothing of shooting anybody whom he took a dislike too, the workers called him the Riga Rattlesnake he was hated, back in the work camp at night Josef would tell the others about this horrible little guy and his abuse of the Polish workers.

Stevie and Yannie were working away tired and hungry as usual, when word came through that there had been a shooting at one of the other work sites, everybody was anxious to know who the unfortunate victim was but it was difficult to get information, communicating was near impossible, any prisoner seen talking was libel to be shot.

Five or six hours later word filtered through that it was the site Josef was working on that the shooting had taken place, the worry for the lads now was who could it be. Their worst fears were confirmed when the word was spread that it was their friend Josef and another lad from their Polish community, the guard responsible was the Riga Rattlesnake. Yannie was disconsolate and vowed to avenge Josef's murder. The story was that Josef's workmate had broken his arm, which left him unable to work a pnumatic machine, the guard had insisted he carry on, waving his pistol in a threatening manner. Josef went to the aid of his injured colleague, he was told to get back to work but defied the guard who raised his pistol and shot him in cold blood, he then turned to the injured man and did the same to him, the bodies were thrown to the side and left until the shift ended. Yannie and Steve never saw their friend again, but they vowed to get even, but first they would need to get close to this guard so that his face would never be forgotten, he had just signed his own death warrant how or when had still to be worked out. The war finished and the two lads surrenderd to the Americans, they were shipped back to Britain where they wanted to voulinteer for the Polish Army but the doctors deemed them unfit, they were sent to a convalacence camp, then finally to Ross-shire where they settled down and married local girls. They often talked about Josef and wondered if his murderer had got his comeuppance, or was he free to enjoy life with no regrets at the number of young men he had dispatched with his pistol, they were sure they would never find out, all they knew about him was that he was Latvian from around Riga but no name.

Back in the Glen Gair labour office the boys had waited near on forty minutes, they were getting fed up listening to Donald Campbell haughing and coughing then depositing the results in the open fire. Suddenly a vehicle screeched to a halt outside the office door, the door of the jeep slammed shut, seconds later the office door flew open to reveal a guy about five foot seven and weighing about twelve stone, Steve could feel the hairs on the back of his neck begin to rise, at the same time he felt Jan sort of stiffen by his side, McGregor stood looking at the two Polish lads before asking where they were from and where they had done shaft work, he seemed quite satisfied and told them they could start work on Monday morning, they would be on a week's trial and if they didn't come up to his standards they would be finished, as he left his parting words were seven am start don't be late. When he was gone old Donald stuck his head round the door and said "I told you he was the most ignorant little bastard you will effer come across", he then invited the lads into his office so that he could get their particulars and allocate them bed spaces in the camp.

Steve and Yannie decided to go to the wet canteen for a beer before setting off back home it was only mid week so no point hanging about, they would return on Sunday afternoon. Stefan ordered the beer, when he returned to the table he could see Yannie was deep in thought so he asked what was on his mind.

Yannie shook his head and said "not a lot" but Steve could read him like a book and persisted until he got an answer. Yannie cleared his throat "Stefan when that guy walked through the door of the office I got a funny sensation. I could feel the hairs standing on the back of my neck like I had seen him before some where" Steve confirmed that he also had sensations along the same lines, they knew Stanislav McGregor was Eastern European but no idea where he was from, but they were sure he was familiar but couldn't put their finger on it.

They left home at midday on the Sunday and caught the bus for Inverness where they would change buses, boarding the Ft William bus at three forty five arriving at their destination around five pm. The bus dropped them at the village shop leaving them about three quarters of a mile to walk to the work camp, they arrived in the camp around five thirty booked in and headed for their bed space the camp sleeping quarters housed thirty men in each hut. As Jan pushed open the hut door they were met by the stench of sweaty feet caused by the guys drying out socks and foot wear ready for their next shift, lots of the guys wore the Donegal socks, this foot wear was so called as it was favoured by the Irish, instead of normal socks the idea was to get a blanket and cut pieces about fifteen inches square, you placed your foot in the middle and wrapped the remaninder round your ankle you held it in place until you wriggled your foot inside your wellie boot. It was a very effective idea but many of the blankets issued from the stores had two fifteen inch squares missing from the corners. The two bed spaces allocated to Stefan and Jan were side by side about half way along the hut most of the other spaces were taken, the guy in the next bed nodded and asked how it was going, Steve said thay were fine and they were starting work in the morning, the guy who was also Polish asked where they would be working, they replied in the shaft. The Polish guy looked at them and said "Vow you goink to vork for the RattleSnake", Stevie was speechless while he tried to retain his composure he was frightened to look at Jan. Jan was the first to respond, "Why do they call him that"? "You vill find out in good time my friend" he spat on the floor and muttered "Vermin"

It was meal time in the canteen so Stefan ushered Yannie out the door of their hut with great haste once they were alone they stopped and lit a fag. Stefan's hand was trembling as he passed the match to Jan. Steve was the first to speak "Yannie I cant believe what has happened to-day, at the moment we are not certain that this is the guy who murdered Josef but it looks like it could be, we need to confirm it, then decided what action to take. We must make sure that we are not incriminated in any way, as I personally don't want to spend the rest of my life in Prison for that low life but he must be taken care of." "We must keep this between ourselves and tell nobody of our background we must be patient." Monday morning and the two Polish lads boarded the truck taking them to the shaft site, the adrenalin was pumping at the thought of meeting up with Mister Macgregor, the journey lasted about fifteen minutes of rather bumpy road, they were all ready to start work dressed in Oilskins and wellie boots and of course safety helmets a must for shaft workers. They no sooner disembarked from the truck than they were confronted by the obnoxious McGregor who told them the name of their charge hand and stressed that the work commenced at seven am be at your post in plenty time, he was the most threatening obnoxious little man they had ever encountered.

The Chargehand asked what experience they had of shaft work he was also Eastern European probably Ukranian he didn't ask where the lads came from nor volunteered to say where he was from it was all very secretive.

He didn't seem to be afraid of Macgregor and shouted back at him when he became obnoxious which was often. The two lads soon got into the swing of things (of course it wasn't rocket science) and the charge hand seemed quite pleased with their work. After a long twelve hour shift the lads would get cleaned up have dinner then head for the wet canteen for a beer, they would find a quiet corner and sit and discuss what they could do about McGregor, they had to avenge their friend Josef's murder, but how. They had established that McGregor was the Riga Rattlesnake by just listening to other Polish lads speaking but they never let on that their paths had crossed before. They had been on the site for six weeks and the shaft was creeping downwards they were approaching the hundred foot mark it was tedious work.

They had worked every week-end from when they had started so on the sixth week they decided to go home and see the family, McGregor was still causing havoc and Jan and Stefan were still at loggerheads as to how they could get rid of this guy who was a torment to everbody he came in contact with. He left the two Polish lads alone as they were good workers and knew what was expected of them, if Yannie had his way he would have whacked McGregor over the head with a heavy iron bar, that would have been the end of him, but Steve was a more patient sort of character and he kept pointing out to his friend if they kill the guy in cold blood no matter what he did in the past they would be charged with murder and probably get a life sentence or worse still, be hanged.

Saturday afternoon was the last production shift until nine pm on the Sunday, the official finishing time on the Saturday was four pm but it depended on when they carried out the last blast if it was around two pm they would be allowed to set off for home early, McGregor who lived in Glasgow went home every Saturday afternoon so he was as keen as anybody to get an early start. I am sure everybody has experienced one of those days where everything goes wrong no matter how hard you try it just goes from bad to worse. The Saturday they were going home turned into one of those days, breakdowns occurring every half hour and the maintinance staff were never in a big hurry to fix things much to the frustration of the guys wanting a flyer. They were running late, McGregor was jumping about like a person demented waving his arms about and being a danger to everybody around him. Every time they executed a blast in the shaft they had to lift all the equipment out otherwise it would get destroyed, this was tedious but essential. Imagine the shaft its like a big dough ring, thirty feet in diameter with a six foot hole down the centre, the centre hole had to be covered when the men were working; for safety reasons, they had an eight foot diameter platform onto which they loaded all the drilling equipment this was lifted to the surface every blast, then there was the three inch diameter rubber hose with a heavy brass coupling through which the compressed air was supplied this also had to be removed. The guys were ready to start lifting out the gear, McGregor was standing at the edge of the shaft shouting and bawling at the men to get a move on, Big Danny Macdonald was the crane driver his banksman was wee Humpy Danny.

Tempers were getting frayed, big Danny stopped the crane and told McGregor to go to hell, he could only work to one banksman and that he was causing confusion. McGregor calmed down and moved futher round the edge. The platform arrived safely at the surface and Humpy Danny uncoupled it, he signalled his driver to lower the rope. Only the air hose, then the two men who had stayed down to hook on the items being hoisted to the surface. The six foot hole was now wide open and the two lads were tethered by their umbilical harness they still had to connect the explosives to the main cable leading to the battery then they would be hoisted clear in a man bucket. They hooked the rope from the crane onto the rubber hose and signalled to the surface to start lifting, it had only gone about six feet when it snagged on the shaft wall, all that was needed was to stop the crane and let the rope go slack, but this was the incident that caused Macgregor to flip he signalled to the crane driver to pull, Big Danny did as he was told. Suddenly the rubber hose came free and shot up the shaft like a catapult just as it hit the surface McGregor looked over the side, it caught him full in the face, he staggered about a bit before disappearing over the edge he was still screaming when he hit the bottom of the shaft some thousand feet below.

The guys were all rough tough workers who had been through the mill, many had witnessed death many times before, but when it happens again a state of shock sets in, maybe they were thinking it could so easily have been one of them, the only noise to be heard was the mournful wailing of the accident alert siren everything else had shut down. The two guys were still down the hole with no means of escape until they managed to get the crane operational again, it was advised to put everything on hold until the police and safety officer arrived. The only instuction given to Yannie and his work mate was to disconnect all the wired up detonators push the wires down the hole and place a stemming bag over them, there was no chance of them blasting that day and if the wires were exposed and there happened to be lightening this could trigger an explosion. The police arrived about an hour later and took photos of the site, Yannie and his mate where shouting that they wanted to be rescued from the shaft it was over two hours since the accident, they were getting a bit fed up as they were still attached to their umbilical harness so they couldn't wander very far. Three and a half hours after the accident the police allowed the crane to be lowered down the hole to rescue the two lads, when ever Yannie rached the top Stefan rushed over and gave him a big hug whispereing in his ear, "I told you patience would pay off, it was a spectacular ending, the other guys who crowded around them had no idea what was going on. Finally at near ten-o-clock the police had taken all the statements and allowed the guys to continue on their way, it would be midnight before they reached Ross-shire but Stefan had a bottle of Polish Vodka in his week-end bag (for a special occasion) so as Danny Macdonald the crane driver drove them home the two Poles and Humpy Danny polished off the bottle of vodka it was a celebration well worth waiting for. The guys were due back on nightshift on the Sunday evening but they had been told to stay home and phone in Monday morning there was no saying when the shaft would get the go ahead, the good news for them was work recommenced on the Monaday morning so their nightshift would start Monday evening.

McGregor's death being a fatal accident there was a court of enquiry and his death was recorded as death by misadventure, he was held totally responsible for his own death. The write up in the news paper explained why he had changed his surname to McGregor. This was his wife's surname and it was quite common for the Eastern Europeans to take their wives names as many of their's were difficult to spell and pronounce. It went on to say how he had been captured by the Germans when his country was overrun and made to work with a slave labour Battalion what they didn't say was that he had volunteered to join the German Army as an NCO overseeing the slave labourers and murdering them when ever the notion took him and his fellow thugs. The Polish lads were satisfied that justice had been done the only thing they wish that he had fallen a few thousand feet further that way the terror he must have felt would have lasted a bit longer.

Powermax had been in the Glen for close on a year and things were beginning to take shape the main tunnel was past the halfway stage. The locals were wishing it would soon end so that they could get back to having a good nights sleep, the explosions from the tunnel were getting weaker the further it progressed but they could still feel the impact it made on the ground so the ones who didn't sleep very sound at the best of times never really manged to get a full eight hours without interuption.

The scheme was good for the Glen, the shop/ post office and the pub showed quite a substantial rise in their takings even although they had a shop and a pub in the camp, basically they only sold essentials and the pub only had a licence to sell beer. The local girls were now used to dancing with guys wearing wellie boots as most of them came straight from the tunnel to the village hall via the pub, some nights there would be a bit of a skirmish but on the whole everybody managed to live side by side without too much friction. Archie Cormack had almost full time work for his small tipper lorry and Dan Fraser's Mini Bus hire company was also flourishing. There were still plenty men requiring lodgings in the village many of them were subcontractors' working on the scheme but not employed by Powermax, they preferred private accommodation in preference to the camp which could get rather rowdy at times especially if the Crown and Anchor gamblers had a fall out. Friday which was pay day, (everybody was paid cash then) would see the (bum boats) arrive at the gate of the camp, this was small vans selling clothes, much of their gear was working clothes and a lot of it was Government surplus, so you would get guys wearing bobbies trousers, an army shirt, airforce pullover and a greatcoat from any one of the three services, this would have been cut just about the middle of the hips, it thus became a reefer jacket.

Fifteen months after starting the main tunnel Powermax reached a major milestone in the contract when the two teams of Tunnelers met in the middle, a halt was called and the engineers marked the tunnel face where they were sure the centre line should be, one driller with a ten foot drill was given the task of drilling a pilot hole, bets were being laid as to how near the centre mark the drill would break through. It was with baited breathe the team of Tunnelers and Engineers waited soon they could hear the hammering of the drill getting nearer then whoosh they broke through and the drill head was less than three inches away from the Engineers markings, quite an achievement after travelling blind for the past fifteen months.

The sad part was that most of the Tunnel Tigers were no longer required, a few stayed to carry on with the tidying up but the majority moved on to pastures new, the local girls could get back to dancing with men wearing leather shoes. Before the Tigers left the Glen, Powermax had supplied a couple of cases of whisky which was the norm at a break through, the four shifts of men had an almighty piss up before breaking up and going their separate ways. There were plenty tunnels being worked throughout the UK and Europe. Powermax were due to complete their contract in nineteen fifty five. Bye the end of fifty six everything was complete the Power Station had been commissioned and was producing power, there was no trace of the contractor, some minor contracts had to be completed but this work was done by smaller contractors who brought in their own employees. The local lads who had by now got used to the Hydro Wages moved on to other Hydro Contacts such as The Orrin and Glen Moriston where work was still in full swing. The Glen Gair scheme had been a boost to the economy, and had left a legacy of about fifteen full time jobs this included the new fish hatchery, most of these posts were filled by local people. There were also three fairly large Timber contractors who owned Sawmills in the Glen, timber was still widely used in the Coal Mines and on the Railways so the Highlands was a thriving place as far as work was concerned. The largest of the Sawmills employed about sixty workers, it was situated about a mile from the village, what had started off as a few bothies to house the woodmen and their families ended up quite a large complex the conditions were primitive but they were a tough breed. Over the years there were some desperado's employed they kept the local police busy especially when they had a fill of fire water, the name given to this rather untidy camp was the O.K. Corral

A new phenomena hit the Highlands in the early fifties in the form of holiday makers, people were better off than they had ever been and things were getting a bit more liberal, young Glaswegians no longer wished to go to the crowded Clyde Holiday resorts, they started branching out, the Highlands became a popular destination, people were earning higher wages, many could now afford a motor car. During the summer months the roads would be jam packed with all sorts, half naked hitch hikers, cyclists, motor bikers, cars pulling caravans and V.W motor homes, the road infrastructure in many areas was still single track with passing places, many an argument took place between a local and tourist who had both passed the passing place nearest them and nobody would budge thus often ending up in a slanging match. A new word enterd the vocabulary of the Highlanders "Nighters" this was the name given to the holiday makers who preferred staying in a house rather than a tent or caravan, the locals jumped on the band wagon and every house with spare accommodation would house nighters it was easy money just clean sheets and a good Scottish breakfast and you were in business. Camp sites were springing up all over the country, anybody with a spare piece of land was entitled to allow campers on and charge them rent for the pitch, no planning permission was needed in the early days in fact many households were still using chemical toilets, the bathroom had not been installed in many premises.

Many foreign tourists also began to spend their summer vacation touring Scotland a major attraction being Loch Ness and the Caledonain Canal.

The scenery may have been spectacular but it had its dangers and quite a few people over the years have lost their lives especially where there are Lock Gates, if anybody fell in the lock their chance of survival was practically nil due to the suction under the gates. One very sad incident that occurred near the end of the fifties happened to three generations of one family. There was the grandmother, father, mother and son in the one car, involved in a mystery that will never be resolved The son had passed his driving test the day before, the family decided to have a drive from Inverness heading to Ft William. At the West end of Loch Oich the road bridge was open to allow a boat through it is part of the Canal System, there were possibly half a dozen cars waiting for the bridge to close, for some reason which will never be known the lad pulled out and overtook the stationary cars straight into the water all four were killed instantly. Nobody ever came up with a reason for this tragedy, it could have been lack of experience on the boys part, maybe sun shining in his eyes. He could have panicked when he saw what was about to happen, why didn't his father shout a warning a mystery that will never be solved and just one of the many tragic accidents to have occurred along the Caledonian Canal?.

By nineteen sixty many changes had taken place the Hydro Scheme was now blended in with the landscape and was producing electricity for the grid, all the houses in the Glen had electricity and most had now installed bathrooms, the tourist trade was still booming with people coming from all over the world, every little cottage had its vacancy sign at the foot of the garden, inside the front door was the visitors book a treasured possesion with many multi national signatures in them.

The timber trade was going well as was the Forestry with a big emphasis on building roads throughout the Forest network to allow more access for the removal of the timber once it was mature.

Into the sixties and the Glen was enjoying all the improvements that modern life was giving them. The villagers had been working hard to raise enough money to build a new village hall, every week there was some sort of fund raising activity and of course they were entitled to a government grant. The full amount required was finally achieved, the Laird donated a piece of land and the committee decided that the best deal was from a company who dealt in pre-fabricated buildings, the plans were drawn up and the building purchased. It didn't take long to ererct and a grand opening week-end was enjoyed by all wishing to get involved.

There were big changes a foot in the education of the children the Government were building further education colleges. The school leaving age was raised to sixteen, when a scholar reached the age of sixteen they could then go to a college and train for a profession. The young people in the Glen soon found out that this new system afforded them better oppertunities, this meant the Foresrty Commision began to suffer and they were ending up with an ageing workforce.

THE COPPER BEECH

Mid sixties and there was a huge road building programme taking place, one such road widening contract was through the village of Glen Gair it was well under way. Donald Macleod was waiting for the County lorry to pick him up ready for his seven am start one morning. The Road Contractor was getting ready to dig into Donalds garden he was aware that he would loose a couple of feet but they had to replace the dyke so he could live with that. As he stood puffing his pipe along came a small pick up and a couple of guys jumped out. They started to remove a chainsaw from the back of the pick up, Donald walked along to where they were and asked what they were about to do, pointing at the only tree near the roadside they said they were about to cut it down, Donald near had a fit, this tree was the pride and joy of his garden a huge Copper Beech possibly eighty to a hundred years old and these vandals were about to destroy it. The two woods cutters more or less ignored this havering old tuchter, they had been told to cut the tree down and that was their mission, that was before they realised that this local fanatic was meaning business, by not allowing them to go ahead, he told them to fetch the resident engineer and he would be told in no uncertain terms what was going to happen. With that the County lorry appeared, Alex Dubh wound down the window. He asked what all the commotion was about, Donald explained what was about to happen, but he was determined it would not go ahead. He told his work mates to go, carry on without him until he had sorted this out, in the mean time he parked himself at the base of the tree thus making sure nobody could fell it behind his back. The two disgruntled wood cutters jumped into their pick up and sped off, while this damned pest of a man was holding them up it was costing them money. Donald sat at his lesiure and had a good puff at his pipe he needed the smoke to keep the midgies at bay, an hour later the Company Land Rover pulled up and out jumped the Resident Engineer when he saw the middle aged man sitting at the foot of the tree he dropped his authoritive mask and thought he better treat this with respect. He introduced himself as Jim Campbell R.E and asked Donald Macleod what the problem was, Donald always the polite man addressed his much younger confrontee. "Weel Mester Campbell its like this, in front of us we have the most beautiful tree that nature could possibly give us, probably older than our combined ages and your men were just about to end its life with the stroke of a power saw, I don't think this vandalism is necessary."

Jim Campbell was squirming and felt uncomfortable, "First of all who am I talking to"? Donald held out his hand and introduced himself as Donald Macleod and pointed out the tree in question was just inside the boundry of his garden. "What's more Meester Campbell nobody has asked my permission to remove the tree." Campbell was again feeling uncomfortable, this old guy was correct the line of the New Road just missed the tree by six or so inches, He told Donald he would put the felling of the tree on hold until he had made more enquiries, Donald asked if he had a sign he could erect just incase it was felled by mistake.

When Jim Campbell arrived back at the tree with a labourer to erect a sign he had to smile to himself, Donald Macleod was taking no chances nailed to a post was a sign saying, This tree is private property do not touch. Jim Campbell had discussed the situation with the Council clerk of works and it was decided the Copper beech would remain untouched, Donald Macleod maintained it would be extreme vandalisim to have removed such a wonderful gift of nature.

The Building of the New Road lasted just under two years, sadly it was to be the last major project in the Glen, but the face of the Glen was changing and with every new idea or rule or regulation the Glen folks were moving on from the old way of life. The raising of the school leaving age and the fact that the teenagers could now enter futher education and attend one of the New Colleges that was coming into operation was a major change for the inhabitants of the Scottish Highlands. Before this new era came into being the teenagers would reach their fifteenth birthday, leave school on the Friday, the boys would start work with the Forestry and the girls would start in one of the near by hotels or maybe the Forestry Nursery depending on vaccancies, that would be their stall set out for life, but the changes had turned everything upside down. Some of the teenagers had to stay in digs all week only home from Friday evening until Sunday evening. In nineteen sixty six ten teenagers reached the age of sixteen, eight of them left the Glen to study further education two of the boys started work in the Glen one was the son of Alex Dhubh, he started with his father as a Council Road Squad worker, Stroopak had retired thus creating a vacancy.

CHANGES AFOOT

The other young lad was the Grandson of Archie Cormack his father had started up a contracting business so he managed to get work with his father. Three of the other boys joined the Merchant Navy/Royal Navy, one other became an apprentice joiner, two girls went to College to study hair dressing and two to train as Chefs. This caused problems for the local businesses i.e., the Hotels were no longer getting the pick of the bunch, they eventually had to employ foreign students for the summer season. With the youth of the Glen away from home most of the week, sporting activities were few and far between, a keen intrest in football was evident after Celtic had won the European Cup ninety percent of the Highland population wore Celtic Tops, but the native sport of Shinty was virtually unheard of. Glen Gair had, had a successful Shinty team before the war but the intrest had dwindled away until none of the locals showed any interest, although in other parts of the Highlands there was at least two leagues with the dominant teams being Newtonmore and Kingussie, another killer of the sport would more than likely have been the Hydro Schemes most men worked eight hours on a Saturday and twelve hours on week days not leaving a lot of time for sport. Highland Games venues were starting to pick up most were Amateur so most of the atheletes were local to the Great Glen, in the mid sixties Glen Gair decided to revive their intrest in the stageing of a day of Highland Games the first attempt was very successful so it became a fixture on the calander.

By the end of the sixties another phase of the Council Housing Scheme had been completed, all the young couples in the Glen were now housed in modern houses and most of the older properties had installed modern facilities such as electric lighting, heating and bathrooms so the old style of living was slowly being eroded. The only reminder that a huge Construction site had once blighted the landscape was the Dam and Power Station but both blended in with the surrounding rock formations so they really enhanced the scenery.

One man had remained in the village after the Scheme was completed, he was an Irish fellow, Patrick Ryan a native of Donegal, Paddy had been sent to Glen Gair to carry out small contracts relating to the Hydro Scheme he was the ganger over a small squad of men. They had to find lodgings which were plentiful in the village especially if it was outwith the tourist season. Paddy managed to make himself comfortable with Bella Campbell a widow who lived in one of the crofts on the south side of the river, he fairly made himself comfortable with Bella who had a couple of teenage sons, with-in a year of moving in he had proposed and they were married. Paddy was a creature of habit he worked hard all week, then on Saturday evening on the stroke of five-o-clock he would be waiting for the pub to open, he would park himself on a stool at the end of the bar and proceed to fill himself to the neck, before chucking out time he would be legless but would manage to stagger home and no doubt catch the wrath of Bella's tongue. Come Sunday morning Paddy would be up bright as a button at the crack of dawn, he would dress and attend mass, a routine that never varied during the many years he lived in Glen Gair.

A new phenomena was sweeping the country, down south they had been on the go for years now the Highlands were starting to catch up with the opening of Supermarkets. The Glen Gair folks most of whom had access to a motor vehicle would travel to Inverness or Ft William. Most people owned fridges and freezers, they could buy enough goods to last anywhere up to a month, even taking into account the price of fuel it was much cheaper than using the local shop or the mobil shops that were still on the go.

The Supermarkets had a detrimental effect on the small shops many of them would not survive, there was a rush to get rid of them, they were being taken over by new owners mostly foreign nationals Indians or Pakistani's but it was a dying business and after many changes of ownerships the Glen Gair shop finally closed, the only way the foreigners made them pay was to stay open practically night and day, another earner was to obtain a licence to sell booze. With the closing of the Glen Gair Shop this presented an opportunity for the owner of the Filling Station to expand his business he immediately took over selling the daily papers, milk, bread and other essentails, this probably saved the Filling Station because selling fuel alone was not a lucerative business.

Glen Gair was normally a very easy going place, life just ambled on, people went about their business and nothing very exciting happened, people died, people got married, babies were born and so the merry-go-round of life kept going. Then suddenly early one morning the early risers were treated to something different, across the river on the South Crofting side two police cars were heading up the Glen it was just after seven am. The first thoughts were poachers, not unusual in this part of the world, either after salmon or deer, necks were craned as they tried to follow the destination of the cars, halfway along the road the two cars pulled up, two policemen got out, opened the gate and headed towards Bella Campbells house, what could be wrong.?

As the Forestry workers gathered to await their transport speculation was rife as to why the cops were about this early, and even more intriguing was the fact that one of the cars was from Ft William something serious must have happened. Somebody suggested that either Paddy or Bella had died suddenly, somebody else pointed out that if that was the case the local bobbies would handle it and there would be a doctor present. Then it was suggested that either Paddy or Bella had murdered one or the other, either that or else somebody had broken in and murdered the two of them so the speculation went on with everybody adding their own theory until a best seller could have been written about the incident. The Police were still there when the Forestry men and the County men left for work, without a clue as to what had taken place at Bella Campbell's croft. Getting on for ten-o-clock there was movement around the croft so the binoculars were fetched and many eyes gazed on the house where they witnessed Paddy being escorted to-wards the Ft William car. Of course the rumour mongers were soon in top gear as they chastised poor Paddy calling him for all the dirty rotten Irish Pigs, any man who would murder a defenceless old woman didn't have a lot of guts in him so hell mend him was the verdict. The main topic in the Glen was the incident that had taken place early that morning, any two people who chanced to meet would spend a little time discussing what should happen to the offender.

Just after two in the afternoon the Postmistress nearly passed out when she sensed somebody standing at the small glass counter, she looked up and was confronted by Bella Campbell, the person they all thought had been murdered. Mrs Keith felt quite faint, she was stuck for words, she had just received a tremendous shock, when she managed to compose herself. She asked Bella if everything was all right as they had witnessed the presence of the Police early that morning. "Ach aye its just that Paddy has some sort of disagreement with the Income Tax people so the Police need him to answer some questions, they thought it would be easier for him to go to the Fort,but I'm expecting him home later in the day". It turned out that Bella would have a long wait as Paddy was detained in custody pending an appearance at the Sheriff Court for Tax Evasion he was eventually tried and sentenced to nine months in prison. Well at least it had provided a bit of excitement and of course provided feed for the gossip mongers but as with everything else in life it was soon history. Paddy served six months of his sentence and returned to Bella as if nothing had happened, he returned to his job with the Forestry Road squad, his first week-end of freedom followed the old routine as before. All Saturday evening in the bar drunk as a monkey by closing time, never interfered with anybody a very inoffensive man.

Glen Gair had been at its peak all through the sixties and seventies everybody was employed. Duncan Cormack's Construction Company employed a few of the younger men, a big part of his business was Plant Hire and of course the Forestry still employed quite a few of the older men. The Forestry Nursery had closed down but with the hotels around the Glen doing good business all summer most of the females were in steady employment for a good part of the year, especially during the fishing and shooting seasons.

THE DEMISE OF THE GLENS

Life seems to be lived in cycles, that seemed to be what was happening in the Highland Glens, for forty years after the War ended if you drove through a Highland Village you were almost certain to see Forestry Commission vehicles parked in drives along the street, the transport used to take the workers to their place of work, the Forestry were huge employers. But things were changing, the East Coast was the place to be that's where all the Oil related work was taking place although there were a couple of Construction Yards on the West Coast. Most of the older Glen Gair men had retired and a few were no longer with us. The Council no longer looked after the roads, this function had been tendered out to Agencies supposedly a cheaper way of keeping the roads in good order, this in the long run turned out to be false economy. Over the years the roads deteriorated to such and extent that the Government had to put aside one hundred million pounds to repair pot holes, I am almost certain if the old methods had still been maintained where the local men continually patched the roads, kept the culverts clear and cut the verges we would not find ourselves with the headache that the British roads have become. Just think how many small road squads a hundred million pounds would pay for, but this is progress?. The next to start chopping the work force was the Forestry Commission once a forest is planted and the roads for extraction are complete I suppose there is not much that needs looking after therefore fewer men are required, again any work that was required was handed over to agencies who work with the bare minimum of staff, they in turn employ many self employed workers where ever it is feasible, so the Forestry is only a skeleton of its former self. Reading the book the Foresters it states that in two thousand and nine there were still seven thousand people employed directly by the Forestry Commission and three thousand Agency Staff this is still a formidable work force. Another major employer was the North Of Scotland Hydro Electric Board but as the years progressed and modern technology advanced the Power Stations which normally required twenty four hour manning seven days a week started to be remotely controlled this meant that one Central Command Post could control the whole system thus reducing the work force by hundreds.

Glen Gair was turning out to be another Highland Glen with many of its population elderly and not many young people coming along to fill the void left as the older generation started to fade away. Donald and Mhari Macleod had gone and only one of their four offspring's remained in the Glen, this was typical of what was called moving on, some of the families had moved out en-bloc with maybe only the elderly parents still staying on in the family home, when they passed away the house would be sold. Many of the families now living in the Council Houses were White Settlers who had been re-housed from other areas, of course if they came from a town they would bring their bad townie habits with them, in most cases it was drugs, the drug culture was just starting to take hold. Glen Gair had been drug free until a Hippy Family were allocated a Council House, every week after they received the Giro the house would be inundated with fellow hippies and druggies from the town, for the next forty eight hours the neighbours would be subject to loud music and loutish behaviour until the police were called, they would scatter the intruders and peace and quiet would descend until the next blow out.

The residents committee were soon up in arms and called a meeting, the local police sergeant was requested to attend the meeting.

After a long drawn out debate as to how to tackle the unsociable behaviour it was suggested that the police should raid the house, the police sergeant pointed out that this was quite difficult to arrange as they didn't have a firm date as to when the next shindig would take place. It was decided that when the people started to gather at the house the police

would be alerted. The committee chairman was given a hotline number
for the drug squad, as soon as this number was activated it would set the
wheels in motion for a full blown drugs bust. For the next six weeks all
was quiet the druggies would frequently disappear the house would be
empty for days on end, the reason for this was that their orgies were held at
different venues, the residents of the Cresent were delighted when someone
else was lumbered with the problem. Then true to form mid afternoon one
Friday, obviously after the benefits had been paid out the weirdo's started
to arrive in dribs and drabs, obviously it was Glen Gair's turn to host the
latest get-together. It wasn't too long before the music started and men
well under the control of some unknown substance were sitting around
the garden smoking evil smelling hand rolled cigarettes, as the drugs began
to take effect all caution was thrown to the wind, soon they were that
stoned they didn't even bother going into the house to use the toilet, they
just whipped it out and peed where they were standing. It didn't take long
before the police were inundated with complaints and the hotline was duly
activated. The antics of the revellers soon brought a storm of protests from
neighbours, with some of the younger guys threatening to go and sort
them out, they were warned against this as there was some danger involved.
The druggies had their usual array of fearsome pets such as two Alsatians
and a brutal looking Rottweiler, it was decided that maybe they would be
better to leave it to the police to handle. These people were the most anti
social human beings imaginable and they continued well into the night,
loud music and the boom, boom of the drums could be heard a mile away,
eventually sleep must have overcome them and peace and tranquillity
descended some time though the night, still no sign of the police.

Alex Dubh was the sole survivor of the people born in the Glen at
the start of the twentieth century, he had been old enough to fight in the
First World War but due to bad eyesight that forced him to wear glasses
as thick as the arse of a jam jar he failed the medical. He had gone on to
marry, they had two of a family, Jeannie the wife had died a few years ago,
Alex stayed with his son and his wife they had moved in when Jeannie had
taken ill. Alex was a very well read man who could talk about events from
all over the world and liked nothing better than a Ceilidh with people who

could enlighten him with subjects he knew very little about. Alex had never left the Glen he was nearing ninety and he could count the times he had visited the town on one hand he was quite content reading or now that Television was available he enjoyed watching sport and general knowledge programmes and the daily news bulleteins. Even when the daughter married an Englishman from around London Alex reluctantly agreed to travel down to see them but only made the journey once. Although he liked and got on well with his daughter—in-law they had an on going feud about his habit of rising at five am every morning.

Because his hearing had deteriorated with age he was quite noisy and had the whole household wakened far too early. But it was an old habit, early to bed early to rise. In the summer Alex could be seen poking about the garden long before six am admiring his lovely show of summer flowers, removing a weed here and there.

This particular morning Alex was sitting on his garden seat looking to-wards the Council Houses and wondering how the druggies were feeling, they had kept the village awake until the early hours, so much for the Police sorting them out as far as Alex was aware the cops were a no show. As he sat and studied his surroundings he thought he detected movement along the river path it was about a hundred and fifty yards away, maybe a Roe Deer or a Fox, he looked hard at the spot and was amazed to see it was an Alsation Dog, holding onto the lead was a huge Policeman creeping along the path. Alex followed the line of the path to where he could see a layby two or three hundred yards to the west, his eyes near popped out of his head when he spotted a Police Mini bus, dismounting from the bus were about six or seven police men and women they were getting dressed in riot type gear. Alex got all excited he had seen this sort of scenario on the television especially when there was trouble in London or one of the other big cities but for it to happen in Glen Gair was something to behold Alex was fair mesmerisied and sat rooted to his garden seat, damn, he wished he had had the binoculars, he would have had a closer look, he didn't want to move incase he missed anything. He swivelled his eyes past the Council Houses to where the riverside path re-appeared form behind the houses, lo and behold another squad of cops, Alex was beginning to think it was some sort of exercise, he had never witnessed anything like it before, they were up to something. It suddenly dawned on the old fellow they were going to raid the house where the druggies were holed up, cute thinking on the part of the police catch them when they are sleeping, old Alex had a grandstand seat. He seemed to be the only human being up and about that morning, the Glen was dead quiet except for the birds chirping away as they flew back and forth no doubt feeding chicks, the adrenalin was beginning to kick in as the cops started to close in on the druggies abode, at least six cops and two dogs were nearing the back enterance, there must have been a pre rehearsed signal because as the cops at the back of the house crept through the gate the ones at the front started to run, both sets arrived at the same time, two whacks with the big red persuaders and the doors were open. The peace and tranquillity of the Glen was completely shattered by the noise coming from the house, soon bleary eyed neighbours were sticking their heads out the windows, ones who were already up made their way into their gardens as they came to terms with what was happening. It took all of about twenty minutes for the noise to abate between barking dogs and cops shouting at the top of their voices along with the screams of the female occupants it is doubtful if anybody in the Glen could still be asleep. Soon the cops started to empty the house first out were the druggies dogs, muzzled and tethered with strong chain leads. Then sadly the next to appear were four young children the two police women took them to a car and sped off in the direction of the town. The children taken care of next came the women five in all, handcuffed and led out to the Black Maria, finally ten men who were made to lie on the ground until more police transport arrived, with-in an hour they were all in custody.

Time for the drug squad forensic team to start their search, by the time they were finished the house would need a complete renovation. Alex Dubh had sat transfixed for well over two hours hardly able to believe the drama that had unfolded before his eyes, as he re-told the story to anybody who cared to listen he would say it was just like watching Down Town Chicago on the television. For the cops its had been a successful exercise with lots of drugs being siezed and better still at least two of the one's arrested were well known drug dealers, it was now a matter of time waiting on the court case to come up. The residents of Glen Gair could look forward to a more peaceful lifestyle once again. A meeting was called and the Council were told in no uncertain terms that druggies were not welcome in this part of the world.

A new name started to appear in many parts of the Highlands especially if there was a good supply of clean clear water near bye. Marine Harvest, seemed to be taking over, their business was Salmon Farming, they would eventually create many hundreds of jobs, their bussiness was a world wide Organisation, they were good for employment but they were also very good sponsors especially for sport, probably due to Marine Harvest, Scotland's other National Sport Shinty got a new lease of life, this along with modern day Governments giving grants to pay for upgrading playing fields and facilities, none more so than Glen Gair. Originally the only piece of ground with grass was behind the council houses it was a sort of play park not very big and quite uneven not suitable for playing any ball games as it was too close to the river and many balls floated away and were never seen again, but with government grants and local fund raising they were able to build a full size Shinty Pitch. They then formed a men's team and a ladies team and they competed in the leagues sponsored by Marine Harvest. Most Saturday afternoons many of the Highland villages have their own Shinty Matches.

There are now six Shinty Leagues the Premier League sponsored by Scottish Hydro has the ten top teams, the other five leagues are sponsored by Marine Harvest three in the North and Two in the South. The Premier League is usually dominated by Kingussie, Oban Camanachd or Ft William they normally have the strongest teams. The Camanachd Cup is the main competition other than the league this is always keenly contested, culminating eventually in the Camanachd Cup Final this can be held in any of the major competing teams home grounds i.e. An-Aird Ft William, Bucht Park Inverness, The Dell Kingussie, or Eilan Newtonmore, Anniesland Glasgow or Oban, as well as the shinty final there is normally a kind of whisky Olympics where many of the spectators get fue. Another big day out for the Shinty Faternity is the yearly Shinty/Hurling match against a team of Hurlers from Ireland, it is a home and an away fixture always a keenly contested affair with blood being spilled on occasions.

It would now be over thirty years at least since the last Council Houses were built in Glen Gair, many of them are occupied by incomers or as Auld Alex Dubh would have called them White Settlers. But people in the Highland Glens were no longer interested in poky wee Council Houses they were more interested in building houses to their own specification, this resulted in new private houses springing up all over the place, huge houses that must cost an arm and a leg to keep warm in the winter.

As well as the cost of building the house the plot or site had to be purchased and the prices being quoted for these often worthless pieces of land were mind boggling anything from fifty to one hundred thousand pounds. In my eyes this is pure daylight robbery because in the first place the ground was worthless but when you get people willing to pay why not exploit them, make a killing while the goose is laying the golden eggs. The strange thing was that people were willing to pay just to obtain the site of their choice.

A NEW CENTURY

As life in the Glen moves on, we were nearing the end of the twentieth century drastic changes were about to happen, there was lots of rejoicing and money spent ushering in the the twenty first century, would it be all it was being cracked up to be. Because of the amount of work always available in the Highland Region from the end of World War Two until the year two thousand, I refered to these years as the Klondike years, one door would close and another would open, there was always plenty oppertunities to make a decent living. But looking around Glen Gair now, there was little eveidence that once over a thousand men had been employed in the Glen as they strove to Construct two major Hydro Electrict Schemes, all that was now visible above ground was the Power Stations and of course the huge Dams, but they were so well planned out that they more or less blended in with the surrounding landscape. Now there was nothing, most of the jobs had disappeared, closed down, in some cases over taken by modern technology. By the Millennium most of the old people who were the backbone of the Glen just after the war were now deceased, very few of their decendants still remained as residents of the Glen. Firstly the old Estate which had been the main employer before and shortly after the war had been sold off, the Lairds family preferred the bright lights of London to the lonely Highland Glen where they had been raised, the only living relative still with an intrest in the Glen was an elderly spinister daughter who maintained a few acres of land, her main interests were horses, she had one hired hand who did most of the work around the place, the rest of the Estate had been sold to the Forestry Commision and now sported mature trees, they would soon be felled and shipped to the chipboard factory between Inverness and Nairn the ground would then be replanted with fast growing timber possibly Spruce. The Hydro Board had also purchased a few acres of the Glen to house their Hydro Projects this included the river which had been rented out to fishing parties during the season, but as with many government owned assets they were eventually sold off to private fininaciers who through letting agents rented out beats on the river to well off syndicates. The Home Farm which covered about two hundred acres was also privately owned this had also been part of the Estate but again sold off probably to pay for death duties, the Hotel another asset of the estate sold off and now privately owned. The other major employer the Forestry Commision was all but defunct many of the older generation had spent their working lives with the Commision. Glen Gair had had its own Forester and an Assistant Forester, there was a Foresters Bungalow and Forestery Offices where one female employee carried out all the administrative duties, then there was the foot soldiers who kept the forests in good shape, planting,draining and then brashing the mature trees. Sadly this has all but disappeared most of the work is done when required by agencies and what I find with agencies they only supply a sort of sticky plaster in other words carry out the miniumn of whats required to keep things going, this comes back eventually and bites them on the back side because the next time repairs are required it will probably cost a lot more than if the job was done properly the first time round.

Into the new Millennium and the Glen looked nothing like it did before the war. The West end of the village had been transformed and now houses the Cemetery, a Shinty Field and a brand new Community Centre. The old Village Hall which had been built in the early sixties was a prefabricated building erected by a company called Doran's they were popular in the sixties because they specialised in pre-fabricated structures. A forty year life span was less than what you would have expected, but it was affordable at the time. The New set up was partly funded by the Scottish National Heritage Society. They have a part of the building which houses the Glen Gair history and artifacts from bye gone days, it is looked after by a team of volunteers who give their time freely helping the tourists find their way around the Glen, they also make sure the history of the Glen is not forgotten.

The Shinty Field is also used fairly regularly as Glen Gair play all their home games on the field, there is also a strong ladies team and various youth teams, on top of this Glen Gair is often the venue for games that have to be played on a neutral ground. Once a year the Highland games take place another stern test for the playing surface especially if there has been heavy rain.

Near bye the Community Cemetery is situated by the river, there are many well kent names on the grave stones some of them of a very young age. The face of the Glen had changed considerably over the past fifty years or so, most of the small estate cottages have been transformed and had huge extensions added, in some cases they look rather unsightly but on the whole they added much needed space and blended in with the modern mansions that are the norm of the present day.

The population had remained pretty steady even given that there was virtually no employment, as I said previously most of the young ones on reaching the age of sixteen elected to go to college to learn a skill. The lucky ones such as apprentices would be hired by various companies and allowed time off to study in college. The galling part was that as soon as they were qualified they would be lost to the glen as the only jobs to suit their qualifications were in the towns or cities so you had an array of skilled people who were no longer staying in the Glen, they only made appearances at the week-end or family get-to-gethers. There were Hair Dressers, Joiners, Mechanics, Electricians, Engineers and a whole host of Qualified Hotel Staff, all sadly now left the Glen living and working else where.

Bye the middle of the first decade of the new century there were very few of the original Glen inhabitants left, the majority were white settlers as the old people would referr to them, people who had moved to the glen for various reasons, one of the main ones being housing, then there were all sorts of arty types like Artists, Authors, Potters, Wood Carvers and of course Bed & Breakfast establishments. Gone were all the Sawmills with their

Bothy Accommodation, no doubt Health and Safety would have killed off this nomadic but happy way of life, but it did keep families fed and a roof over their heads. The decendants of the original families were few and far between and there was little chance of reversing the trend people needed to work so that they could earn money to pay for the daily needs.

It was getting expensive to live in places like Glen Gair especially for the ones who had to travel to work, the price of fuel was starting to rise and seemed to be running out of control.

THE LATEST WHITE SETTLER

Aileen Grimshaw breezed into Glen Gair like a breath of fresh air, well she was driving a clapped out V.W Mobile Home which held all her worldly possesions, she had just landed a job with the Highland Education Authority as a relief teacher. Aileen was a bit of an eccentric dressed in a Tartan Shirt and the latest fad in trousers, the very versatile Cargo Pants, she had fallen in love with the Highlands through a quirk of fate and her ambition was to eventually set up home in one of the picturesque Highland Glens and here she was in Glen Gair.

Aileen was a Londoner born and brought up in Bermondsey, she had been a very good scholar and eventually attended a teacher training college where at the age of twenty one she qualified as a teacher, by the age of thirty she was deputy head of the school. She had a great love of the outdoors, at every opportunity she would jump on a cross channel ferry and head for France where she would spend her time hiking and exploring the country side, eventually she formed a ramblers club and encouraged young people to follow her persuits.

The Club had ventured into Wales and even managed a trip to Ireland but it never crossed her mind to try Scotland, believing that it never stopped raining and it was always very cold. As the years passed her by she started to become very disillusioned with teaching, every class in the London Schools was multi national, the children were quite disruptive, a big problem being the parents, many of whom could not speak proper English, if at all, communicating was difficult and often frustrating. To chill out Aileen always tried to have her Friday evenings in a pub somewhere, preferably if she was at home in her Local, she would have a few beers and enjoy the company in the bar for the evening, she was often propositioned by members of the opposite sex, she was quite a looker and her dress sense could be rather provocative at times ie short skirts and showing a lot of cleavage but it didn't bother Aileen and she never got herself involved.

One Monday morning she turned up at the school well ahead of time and was sitting having a coffee when her boss arrived. Mike Smythe was getting on a bit and starting to look forward to retirement, teaching was not what it used to be, the lack of disipline was getting worse as the years rolled bye. He sat down after the usual banter with his deputy, the secetary brought him a cup of coffee and some mail which she laid on his desk. He looked at Aileen and asked if she would mind taking assembly that morning as he had some other business to attend to. Assembly usually lasted twenty minutes, Aileen returned to the office after answering a few questions asked by her colleagues, she had been away for forty odd minutes, when she returned, Mike looking over his half moon glasses asked if everything was ok she nodded her head and said "Yes everything is in order". He drummed his fingers on the desk (one of his many annoying habits) "Are you doing anything intresting from Wednesday until Friday" he asked. Aileen hesitated for a minute then shook her head waiting in anticipation as to what her boss would throw up next. "How do you fancy a little jaunt to Glasgow"? he asked, Aileen's was all eyes and ears as she listened to what he had to say. "There is a seminar at the SECC in Glasgow we have an invite for either one of us to attend but I have other commitments so the invitation is yours if you are available."

Aileen was ecstatic three days away from the jungle as she called the school, finally a chance to visit Scotland all for free, she felt like jumping up and giving Big Mike the hug of a life time but that would not be a proper way for his deputy to behave.

She received her instructions, board the Glasgow shuttle from Heathrow at seven pm on Tuesday evening, arrive Glasgow eight fifteen, bus into the city centre, then taxi to the Hilton Hotel, she could hardly contain herself. After allowing her time to digest the itinerary Mike Smythe told her he expected a full report on his desk next Monday morning along with any bumph handed out at the Conference. Tuesday evening Aileen found herself racing along the runway as they started take off from Heathrow, they had an uneventful journey and were soon fastening their seat belts as they prepared to land, it was a beautiful sunny evening and Aileen probably saw Glasgow at its best. It was just after nine when she arrived at the very impressive looking Hilton Hotel, she gave her name and the school she was representing and with very little fuss after registration she was allocated a room, she was told that there were sandwiches available in the lounge. She dumped her case had a look round the room and at the view from her window, it was mostly motorway, then she decided to have a bite to eat as it was getting quite late. As she stepped from her room it happened to be exactly the same instant as the woman in the next room she was rather large, as they turned to face each other the big lady asked Aileen if she was here for the seminar Aileen nodded and answered "Yes". Before Aileen could move a huge hand had grasped hers and was being pumped up and down as the lady introduced herself as Katie Foulbister from a school in Shetland. She asked Aileen if she was going for a sandwich, again Aileen nodded and answered "Yes" so the two of them set forth in search of the grub by the time they found it Aileen was totally confused and thought to herself it was far easier to understand the Pakistani women in Bermondsey than this huge Highland woman. They found the food and coffee and sat at one of the tables, big Katie rambled on Aileen shaking her head or else nodding not sure if it was in the right place or not, she had never ever heard this accent before and the words being used was like a foreign language. But she seemed to be a nice homely person, after forty five minutes of severe ear bashing they decided to go to their rooms Big Katie arrived first, just as Aileen was about to open her door the Big one asked if she fancied a night cap before turning in, after some persuasion Aileen agreed to keep Katie company as she had her night cap. Aileen sat down on the only chair as Katie rummaged in her case, she produced a Bottle of Highland Park whisky and a box of short bread, Aileen screwed her nose up at seeing the whisky, she remarked she often drank Brandy but had never tasted whisky. Katie poured substantial drams and then proceeded to coach her visitor on how it should be drunk. "Dinna tak a big houp at it, jist wee sooks and ate the short breed at the same time and I'll gaurantee you'll sleep like a log." Aileen was completely bamboozled as she neither understood houps or sooks so she just sipped in small quantities until her glass was empty,she declined a second and excused herself as she left for bed. She had taken a bit of a shine to Big Katie if only she could understand a bit more of what she said to her.

Ready for bed Aileen was feeling a little queasy she was not used to drinking Scotch Whisky and was quite thankful that she had only had the one, they had to be at the Conference Centre at ten am sharp and she would have to depend on Katie to show her the way, thankfully Katie would have to stop talking while the speakers were in action.

Aileen had booked an early call for seven thirty, she was still asleep when it came through causing her to wake with a start, near jumped out of her skin, she had a stretch then headed for the shower.

Bye quarter past eight she was ready for breakfast, just as she was about to leave there was a tap on her door, Katie announced she was on her way to eat she waited until Aileen had joined her, they then caught the lift down to the dining room. Aileen was quite a light eater at breakfast time and opted for some fresh fruit and scrambled egg. Her eyes near popped out of her head when Katie arrived back at the table with a plate of porridge and a full Scottish breakfast, she had to ask about the tattie scone, not a London delicacy, by the time Katie had demolished her mammoth feed it was getting close to nine-o-clock they would need to get a move on.

Aileen was hugly impressed with the SECC Site, they were not in the main Auditorumn but there were about two hundred and fifty teachers seated in a smaller theatre type building. The guest speaker that morning was a professor from the Caledonian University he rambled on a bit mostly about disipline or maybe it should have been lack of it, anyhow the first session lasted until twelve thirty, then they broke up for lunch, there were snacks available so Aileen and Katie grabbed what they could and headed for the out doors they would have another two and a half hours cooped up in the afternoon. Although the two ladies had been in each others company since yesterday evening they had very little time to talk about their back grounds and circumstances but it didn't take Katie long to start telling her history, her cue was when Aileen asked what her husband did, she had already sussed out that she had two of a family, Katie seemed to have all the vices that are available one being that she smoked, not a lot but she liked a good drag. She was just filling her lungs when Aileen asked about the husband, spluttering and coughing she exclaimed, "That b*****d!", "it's a lang story but it has been over for the past fifteen years". "When I was attending Uni in Aberdeen I wis only ever able to get home occasionally, my folks had a small croft and my father also did a bit of fishing to suppliment the income so they were never well off, my bursary was needed to pay for my keep so money was always scarce". "Anyhow near neighbours of ours had a son Magnus he was in the Merchant Navy and only home occasionally, he always had plenty money which he spent like it was going out of fashion, we lived at the back of beyond, the nearest pubs and hotels were in Lerwick, the bold Magnus used taxi's all the time, lots of his visits into town ended in him being drunk but the taxi drivers were glad of his business so they made sure he arrived home safely, his father and him would always be at loggerheads but it was water off a ducks back and Magnus would dissapper for days on end until the flak died down, off course being an only son his mother used to run after him and scold his father for always being on his back".

"One day we were both at home at the same time, I was nineteen and due to graduate as a teacher in about a years time, Magnus had pestered me for a date on numerous occasions but I always said no, you see my parents weren't too enamoured with Magnus's attitude towards his father, for me to go out with him would have been taboo." "Do you want me to continue" Aileen nodded her head and said "Please do" even although she still found Katies accent rather hard to understand at times. "Well as fate would have it we were heading back to Aberdeen on the same boat at the week-end, Magnus bought me a couple of drinks at the bar and then told me he was staying in Aberdeen for a couple of nights before heading for Tilbury Docks in London, would I go out with him on the Sunday evening, after some consideration I decided there would be no harm in agreeing to meet him, nobody from home would ever know."

"We met as agreed and Magnus insisted we would have a Chinese Meal after that we had a stroll around town and after a couple more drinks he walked me back to my digs, he wanted to meet me again the next evening but I declined his offer using my studying as an excuse, although I was tempted, we parted and he left with my address saying he would keep in touch, he had been a perfect gentleman, I couldn't see why my parents had such a downer on him". "Are yea sure yir nae getting bored ?" again Aileen nodded her head and told Katie to contimue. "Well to cut a long story short every time Magnus came home after that we would meet up in Aberdeen and the inevitable happened I fell pregnant, what a bloody prediciment, I had just received my degree and was about to look for a job, telling ma mither and faither would be an ordeal but worse was to come when I had to tell them wha the faither was." Aileen glanced at her watch she had been so intrigued by her friend's story, she didn't notice that time had caught up with them so they had to ajourn Katie's life story until later on, Aileen had to concentrate hard to follow the gist of the story but she was getting there she managed to get Katie to slow down that was an enormous help.

As often happens at seminars some of the lecturers are a bundle of boredom,unfortunately the guy on stage that afternoon had the most awful dreary voice imaginable, this caused a few of the audience to very nearly nod off, his theme was health and safety, the government were about to change the legislation regarding Health and Safety it was information that needed to be taken heed of as the new rules put more onus on the teachers regarding the well being of their charges. Aileen made sure she had picked up all the leaflets covering both sessions, they were back in the hotel for quarter to six, as Katie entered her room she said she would go for dinner in an hour after she had a shower and got changed.

After going over the menu and choosing what they were having to eat Katie asked if Aileen wanted to hear the rest of her life story. Aileen was all ears as Katie started chapter two. "Magnus had just left for a short trip to Holland so the bombshell of me being pregnant would have to wait till he got back." "Then I got a phone call from my mother telling me she had bad news, a near neighbour had been involved in an accident on the croft and had died, I near collapsed when she said it was Magnus's father he had been electrocuted while using a power tool, my blood ran cold this would only add to my troubles". "Later that evening Magnus called he was on his way home and would be in Aberdeen around ten pm.

He asked if I would meet him, he sounded quite calm for somebody who had just been told his father was dead". "I stayed in Aberdeen until the night before the funeral, after it was all over I managed to get Magnus on his own and asked when he would be going back to his ship, he told me he would be going to Aberdeen on Monday to resign his post with the shipping company so he would meet me on Monday afternoon, I found out later he was going to stay home and help his mother run the croft". "Monday afternoon Magnus arrived about four pm he was stinking of booze, anyhow we found a café and over a cup of coffee I told him I was three months pregnant, as usual Magnus showed very little emotions except to say I suppose we'll have to get married". "I burst into tears what a callus brute I still had the ordeal of telling my parents but that didn't phase him either". "We'll get married first and then tell them there's damn all they can do after that". "He just didn't seem to be bothered who got hurt or what the concquences were but that was Magnus a selfish oaf".

"I faced up to my duties and confided in my mother she was most upset and cried for hours,but the damage was done, now for my father, my biggest worry about him was that he would suffer a heart attack, but he took the news very calmly although he stressed that he was far from happy about me being pregnant but more so about the drunken waster who had made me that way, that off my chest Magnus and I got married in the registrar in Aberdeen". "We moved in with his mother in the croft, not an ideal situation but I had no choice, my loon was born six months after I was married but my troubles had only started because I soon found my self expecting again, it would mean twa bairns under a year old what a mess, my girl was born six weeks before the boy's first birthday it was like having twins". "I made up my mind after my girl was born that there would be no more bairns and if Magnus didn't toe the line I would be taking drastic steps to get out

of the predidiment I found myself in". "He continued as if he was a single
man drunk nearly every night of the week, my mother saw how unhappy
I was, she offered me a room for myself and the bairns but I was proud
and independent so I vowed not to give in". Eventually my mother-in-law
and myself were feeding the cattle if not they would starve, further more
the money was running out he was making all our lives a misery with his
drinking and constant rows". "But if you keep battling on and have faith
things will eventually work themselves out, I was peeling tatties one forenoon
when the phone rang, it was an old friend from my college days, she asked
if I would be interested in a teaching job, I was all ears". "They were looking
for somebody to act as a relief teacher to cover schools on the island, if I got
the job I would need to take a refresher course to bring me up to date, I told
her yes I would start to-morrow if possible". "My boy was just started school
and I was confident my mother would take my girl if I got a job so I arranged
the interview and was successful. From there I eventually managed to get a
permenant job in our local school, both kids were now attending the same
school I was teaching in so it was just perfect". "Although I was living on the
croft with Magnus and his mother our marriage was over it had lasted all
of three years, he was diagnosed as an alcoholic, every penny he earned was
spent on drink, I managed to survive on my wages, I had been teaching for
five years when lady luck threw me another life line".

The government had ordered cut backs in the budget, it looked like
our small school might be closed down as we only had fifteen pupils,
after much debate it was decided to send our senior pupils to the new
Academy in town, one post would go I expected the worst but was aware
my head teacher was due to retire shortly. The Authorities offered her early
retirement and then offered me the job teaching the puplis that were left,
nine in all, I would teach them to Primary five, the big bonus was there
was a house available when Mrs Duncan found a place to stay, I couldn't
believe my luck, free from Magnus Foubister at last, from then on I vowed
my life would never again be blighted by a man, for the past twelve years I
have been foot loose and fancy free. Oh there has been men in my life but
nothing permenant. So there you go Aileen my life story in a nutshell thank

you for being a patient listener. They finished their meal went through to the lounge for a night cap before retiring to bed, as they sipped a Drambuie Katie outlined her week-end before returning to Shetland. She had booked into a cheaper Hotel in Renfield street for Friday night she then intended to have a night on the town, there were some very good Folk Clubs where many of the Islanders used to meet up, that was what she intended doing.

Later in the evening around eleven she would go to a Casino where she would have a flutter at the tables until about one a.m. she would then get a taxi back to her hotel, she pointed out that her nights of enjoyment in Shetland were few and far between and anyhow the parents of her pupils might not have approved of Miss having a flutter at the gaming tables so she had to take advatage away from prying eyes. She asked Aileen if she fancied staying for the night, she was sure she could get her room upgraded to double status with single beds, pointing out this would be cheaper than two single rooms, Aileen was quite taken with the idea, she would be three days in Glasgow and hadn't had a chance to have a look round the place so this was maybe an idea, first she would need to see if she could change her ticket as she was due to fly to London on the Friday evening at seven pm, so she would make enquiries in the morning,Katie had planted the seeds. Next morning Aileen phoned the booking office and yes she could get her ticket changed but there would be an admin fee, so the ticket was changed and after the Seminar ended at two pm on the Friday the two ladies made their way to the Hampton Court Guest House in Renfield Street. They had a quick shower and got changed into casual clothes, they would have plenty time to have a wander around the City Centre before they embarked on their evening of merriment. Katie was better than any tour guide and took Aileen on a sort of circular tour, during their walk they came upon the tourist guide premises, Aileen was keen to get some brochures, as she browsed through the glossy suppliments and flyers praising the beauty of Scotland one that caught her eye in the hiking and biking section was the West Highland Way, a seventy eight mile hike through the most rugged scenery in Britain she picked up as many brochures as was available, she would study them more closely later.

Seven pm and the ladies were seated in a Chinese resturant ready to eat, Katie commented that she never often had the chance to eat Chinese as the nearest one at home was fifteen miles away so she always made sure she could indulge when ever the opportunity arose.

By eight-o-clock they were ready to go clubbing, they found a Folk club just off Sauchiehall Street, it was pretty well full up although the music hadn't started, they grabbed a table and Katie headed for the bar, Aileen told her she would only be having a few beers as she wanted to have a clear head for the sight-seeing tour the next morning. Katie was knocking back the Highland Park like she was filling a forty gallon drum. Aileen was enjoying the music and the dancing was something else, although she had heard Scottish Music before this was the first time she had witnessed the natives executing the dances, dead on eleven p.m. Katie announced it was Casino time, although Aileen was born and brought up in the heart of London she had never been in a gambling establishment, in London it was considered that the casino goers were low life or foreign immigrants, decent working class people didn't frequent these places. Big Katie seemed to be streetwise and knew what she was doing, on entering the casino she purchased twenty five pounds worth of chips and proceeded towards the roulette wheel, she asked Aileen if she fancied a try but she declined and said she would watch for a spell then maybe she would give it a go. Katie was going great guns and in the first hour she had doubled her money, she then got a bit cockie and upped her stakes not a wise move, she found herself back where she started, getting near to one am she was winning ten pounds, this would be her last bet so she placed her tenner winning's on the highest odds on the wheel.

The look of astonishment when her number came up, she had won ninety pounds plus her stake not a bad nights work but it was time to head back to the digs, they were both quite tired and of course the alcahol didn't improve matters. Katie still managed to devour a huge full Scottish breakfast next morning as she prepared to show Aileen the sights of Glasgow, they decided to get a ticket for an open top touring bus this was real handy as they could get off and on whenever they pleased. Katie had a brochure highlighting the main places of intrest. Their first stop was the Peoples Palace, then on to The Barras (Aileen remarked they were similar to Petticoat Lane in London), from there it was the Burrel Collection, Glasgow Cathederal and finally they spent the last hour in the Buchanan Galleries. Katie had to catch a train for Aberdeen at five pm, they parted company at four-o-clock Aileen needed to get a coach to the Airport her flight was at seven, as they hugged each other good bye they insisted that they would keep in touch and meet again when ever possible.

In the airport Aileen had time to kill so she wandered around and finally came to a stall owned by the Scottish Tourist Board she picked up a couple of hiking magazines and settled down to absorb the contents. The West Highland Way jumped out at her once again, she was fascinated by the wonderful hike and she made up her mind that she was going to do this hike come hell or high water, she would broach the Ramblers Club when she got back to Bermondsy. She arrived at her Flat just going on ten pm, she had a shower while a Pizza warmed in the oven, after she had eaten she poured a stiff brandy and sipped it down while she caught up with her mail. She went to bed just after eleven and had another browse at her tourist Brochures, she got quite excited when she noticed that near the end of the book there was another hike that took her fancy the Great Glen Way, this was shorter than the West Highland at Seventy three miles she envisaged doing both over two weeks, but just a thought at the moment, she could hardly wait for the meeting of the ramblers club.

It would be interesting to see if any of the others would show the same enthusiasm as she was showing, she felt well and truly hooked.

Next morning was Sunday she would need to get her computer working as she had to write a report for her boss Mike Smythe, no doubt he would be looking for all the I's dotted and the Ts crossed, better not tell him aboot sookin Highland Park as a night cap with Katie Foulbister. It took her most of the day to type up the ten page report, she was still working on her computer skills and could do with speeding up her typing but she was assured it would come with practice. Back in the school rest room on Monday morning she was inundated with questions about her trip to

Glasgow, as she was leaving for her office she dropped the Hiking brochures on the table,commenting that there was some interesting information for the rambling club. She dropped her report on the boss's desk then got stuck into the correspondence that had built up during her three days away, then there was the computer to check she could see her whole morning wasted, much of it pointless notices, many of which didn't apply to her, the down side of having a computer. Big Mike had read her report and called her through to his part of the office, he wanted to go over some of the points raised at the Seminar so that wasted another good hour of her day, before she knew it, it was lunch time, she had achieved practically nothing, paper work and now computers were extremely time consuming.

Aileen always made a point of going to the Staff Rest Room where she could have a good chin wag with her colleagues during lunch break especially the members of the Rambling / Hiking Club, to-day they were full of questions about the brochures she had brought back from Scotland. Tom Hicks was one of the more enthusiastic members and he was all geared up to have a go but Aileen pointed out that to do both walks they would need at least two weeks, the summer holidays looked like the best bet. The main body of the club members would be meeting on Wednesday evening then they could put out feelers as to how many were interested, Old Tom was sitting deep in thought when he asked Aileen "Did you say, The West Highland Way finished in Ft William and the Great Glen Way strated at the other side of the town"? Aileen nodded her head and answered "Yes that's how I interperet the brochures". Tom was a Victor Milgrew look a like and probably just as lively, suddenly he burst into life his brain must have engaged again "Ft William he muttered" then turning back to face Aileen he said, "Big Calum the janitor comes from Ft William, we need to have a chat with him, he will almost certainly be at the meeting on Wednesday". The lunch break ended and they all dispersed to their various offices and class rooms. Aileen was doing her rounds when she bumped into Calum the janitor, somebody must have been bending his ear because right away he broached the subject of the rambling club walking the West Highland Way, he had done it a few times before so he knew what he was talking about, Aileen suggested they meet up after work and discuss the idea before the meeting on Wednesday evening, Calum was all for that, never let the opportunity of having a pint with a lovely lady go past so they decided Tuesday evening at their local seven pm.

Calum was a big lump of a Highlander, he was born and brought up in the shadow of Ben Nevis, it was the first thing he saw when he wakened every morning.

In his younger days he had been a keen sportsman participating in two of the most strength sapping sports imaginable i.e. Shinty and Canoeing. His Canoeing skills were honed in the treacherous waters of the River Nevis where the water barely reached above freezing point all year round, he became so expert that he represented his country in Canoeing slaloms all over Europe. Now his sports were confined to leisurely hiking and the odd game of badminton in the Club Premises in Bermondsey. Calum served his apprenticeship as a Plumber in Ft William, after becoming a fully fledged Tradesman he decided to spread his wings and see a bit of the world setting off with three fellow tradesmen they headed for London. This turned out to be a wise move as they were inundated with work and stuck together for a few months before going their separate ways, mainly due to their involvement with the opposite sex. The first while in London was quite exciting but the shine for the place soon started to wane due to the cost of everything. Also some of the work Calum had to do was quite dirty and unexciting, the job he hated most was clearing blocked drains, they were a regular occurrence. He would arrive at the depot in the morning, his work sheet woud state, blocked drain such and such a street, Calum and his apprentice would jump in the van and head for where ever they were required as soon as they got there they could smell the problem, if it was warm weather it was even worse. As soon as the van stopped they would be confronted by irate citizens, they were of all Nationalities all jibbering away in their broken English, at first Calum would stand and take the abuse but after a while he thought why the hell should I take all the flak and say nothing. He was lucky in as much as that he could speak a little Gaelic so he would let fly at them "Don't you shout at me yea big fat ugly *   *   * bitch its nae my fault your drains are chocked". When they calmed down

Calum would get to work, lift the manhole cover and the culprit would be staring him in the face, Pampers packed solid along with all the other bits and pieces associated with sewage, get the hooks out of the van and start fishing them out he would call the West Indian Women over and point out what was wrong he could never be sure but he often thought they had a red face after the hassle they had given him, he would often remove over forty soiled pampers. Calum soon got to know what choked the drains on each street just by finding out the nationality of the inhabitants i.e. Chinese blocked the drains because they poured used fat down the toilet pan so he became well versed in the blockages of the London street drains. It was always Calum's ambition to tour the world so one day after unblocking his third drain before lunch he thought to himself, bugger this I am fed up being up to my elbows in other peoples shit, I'm taking a year out and doing my world tour. His current girlfriend Mattie couldn't believe what she was hearing when Calum announced he was going home to tell his mother his plans then giving his boss a month's notice and on the first of October he was off, would she like to go with him, she was so taken aback that she struggled to answer, she was told she had four weeks to make up her mind. Calum made the trip to Ft William assured his mother and sister that he would be ok. Back in London he wrote a letter of resignation and handed it to the clerkess at the reception desk, as he collected his work sheets for his days work he was delighted to see he had a job repairing lead cladding on a Church roof, he was hoping it would last a month so that he could avoid any more shitty drains.

When he handed in his work sheets that evening the clerkess shouted that the boss would like a word just go through. He knocked and was told to enter, he got on well with his boss so they were on first name terms. The boss was quite disappointed after reading Calum's letter and sincerely asked if anything was the matter with the job. Calum shook his head and explained that he had promised himself that he would tour the world before he reached the age of thirty, he felt that the time was right to go now. The boss was very understanding and showed his dissappointment at loosing such a competent reliable tradesman but assured him his job would be available when he got back, they shook hands and Calum left. He had to meet Mattie that evening to find out her plans, their usual meeting place was the nearest pub so after a bit of dinner he headed down to the Blue Boar, arriving at the same time as she did, he ordered two drinks and joined Mattie at a table. Callum didn't rest on cermoney and asked, "Well"? Mattie didn't hesitate and said "Yes she had handed in her notice and checked her bank balance so she was ready to go".

The first of October saw the two of them with huge rucksacks standing on the platform of St Pancras Station waiting to board the Eurostar they had managed to get concessionary fares that would take them to Paris, Callum wasn't fussy about wasting time in Europe they could hop over there at any time, he was keen to get to Asia so they headed for Greece and on through Turkey. During his time in London he had worked with and met many people from Sri Lanka, he always found them very sociable people, when he told them he was travelling round the world they told him to make sure he was in Sri Lanka for Christmas it was a wonderful time of year to be there, especially on the South Coast where all the Europeans gathered for the festivities.

Crossing on the jam packed Ferry Boat Calum got talking to some of his fellow European passengers a few of them were from England, they had been coming here for years, their advice to Calum and Mattie was to stay in the North as the South coast was a mad house, over crowded with Brits and Europeans of all Nationalities, they assured the young couple they would enjoy themselves just as well in the North but with much less hassle. They had a little pow wow and decided to take the advice of the wise old heads, soon after arriving they managed to check into a self catering apartment which they booked until the twenty seventh, Calum wanted to bring in the New Year in Thialand. They spent the twenty fourth of Decemeber just exploring around the beach had a few beers, during a stop for lunch they bumped into some of the ferry passengers who invited them to a beach party on Christmas day, it was starting off about four pm. Christmas morning arrived and the twosome exchanged gifts had a long lie then went for a stroll and some lunch. At three pm they started to get ready for the party, about quarter to four they were on their way, bye the time they arrived there was quite a crowd gathered, Calum enquired about who he would pay as there was a huge spread of food. With-in an hour the party was in full swing, a local dance troup appeared and put on a show of Sri Lankin dancing it turned out to be quite an event and of course there was plenty alcohol, as the night progressed so did the level of inebreation in many of the party goers.

By eleven pm Calum was as fue as a whelk, Mattie wasn't far behind him, she decided it was best to get him back to the flat before he got any worse, it was just on mid-night when they collapsed on the bed. When Calum awoke next morning he could hardly breathe, they had forgotten to switch on the air conditioning, he also noticed that there was a lot of noise coming from outside almost like people in distress, he jumped out of bed and switched the clean air on, grabbed a bottle of coke a cola from the fridge looked at his watch and gasped in amazement, it was after eleven am, he now needed something to ease the head, it was bursting, Mattie was lying in a heap under the duvet moaning and groaning like a wounded buffalo. Calum nearly fainted when he switched on his mobile phone and noted that he had fifteen missed messages, right away he thought of his mum back in Ft William hoping she was ok. He started to read the messages they were all pleas for him to get in touch. He called Mattie and asked her to check her phone, with much wailing and moaning she found her phone and switched it on, hers was the same get in touch right away about twenty times.

Calum sent his mother and his sister a text message asking what all the fuss was about at the same time he switched on the television and near had a seizure when he he saw the news the whole of the Indian Ocean had been devastated by an earthquake near the Island of Sumatra thousand of people were missing feared dead, Calum felt a cold shiver run down his spine it could have been them, they would have known nothing about it. Back home in Ft William there was relief as the text message arrived letting them know that Calum was ok and no sign of any damage where they were. In Inverness at three am on Boxing Day morning one of Calums relatives had had difficulty sleeping, so he donned his head phones and

listened to the three am news bulliten, near the end of the three minute
update the broadcaster mentioned that there had been a slight tremor off
Sumatra. Little did he know at that point that two hundred and thirty six
thousand people had lost their lives and that more than half of Sri Lanka
had been washed away drowing holiday makers and locals a like, it was one
of the biggest natural disasters ever recorded. Even though the North of
Sri Lanka had escaped virtually untouched the whole place was in turmoil
and it was later in the day before the full extent of the disaster was realised.
The eruption had occurred at fifty eight minutes past midnight just off
Sumatra it triggered off a tidal wave that eventually petered out near the
coast of America.

Calum's plans were on the back burner the whole area around the Indian
Ocean was in utter chaos nobody had any idea how bad the problem was
for a few day's, there were so many different countries involved, it would
take some sorting out so the best idea was to sit tight and let things take
their own course. On the thirtieth of Decemeber Calum managed to get
transport out of Sri Lanka which eventually took them to Thailand where
they celebrated the New Year.

Next port of call was Australia, they had been on the road for seven
months and were a bit travel weary there was also a financial worry, the Sri
Lanka escapade had cost them a lot more than they had budgeted for so cash
was getting tight, they still had New Zealand and America to visit before
they headed back to London hoping to arrive the last week in September.
Calum decided to try and get a job in Australia just to earn some extra
cash but he had no chance of being a Plumber it was no go due to trade
unions etc. The only thing available was working in resturants washing up
and clearing tables this paid the very minium of wages but it would pay for
their digs and they could eat in the restaurant. The two of them signed on
and did a month of the most boring work imaginable but it did tide them
over during their stay in Oz.

Last week in September saw them back in London, the first thing they
did was part company, things had been a bit iffy for the past couple of months
probably due to being in each others pockets for a whole year, anyhow it
was over, they parted on aimable terms. Calum needed a job he was close

to being broke, the bad news was that since they left London a year ago the building trade has slipped into recession, on top of that the banks and mortgage lenders were playing silly buggers by not lending money, when they did it was at extortionate rates. Passing the Job Centre Calum noted a vacancy for a School Janitor prefably a time served tradesman, Plumber/ Electrician would be ideal. This would suit Calum down to the ground and the wages were in line with Tradesmens rates, hence the reason that Calum became School Janitor at Bermondsy Senior Secondary School.

Aileen kept glancing at her watch as usual she was running behind schedule, she was supposed to meet Calum in the Blue Boar as seven pm, it was nearly eight minutes past and she was still in her flat, a little coat of lippy and she would be on her way. She poked her head round the door of the snug and spotted Calum in the corner he was almost ready for his second pint of Guiness,since returning home he had aquired an Irish girl friend, he had also taken to drinking Guiness to try and impress her father. Aileen said she would get him a re-fill and a drink for herself before she sat down. She apologised for running late and then had a moan about having to use her own time to keep up with her school work, comfortably seated with a pint each they got down to business. Aileen explained that she was keen to do the West Highland Way, then the Great Glen Way. Calum told her he was familiar with the first one, he had done it a couple of times, but the Great Glen Way was only opened in two thousand and two the year he left home but on having said that he was familiar with the route.

Aileen asked if he would be interested in driving the mini bus if they decided to go ahead. Calum was all for it, he had intended to go home and catch up some jobs his mother had on her list of things to do, also to introduce Annie to his family, they could arrange to get it all done on the same fortnight. Calum went on to explain the pit falls of the W.H.W ie the hazards, midgies and rain, he didn't think it possible for a team of townie school kids and an elderly teacher meaning Tom Hicks could do the walk in one week he thought maybe ten days was more realistic. Aileen said she would need to clear the mini bus with her boss Mike Smythe but she didn't see a problem as the school was on holiday and the trip was Educational.

Calums girl friend was coming to meet him at eight-o-clock so they had about forty minutes to sort things out. First they needed to clear the mini bus, if that was oked it was an eleven seater, Calum wanted to take his girl friend with him, that meant there would be nine seats left, Aileen decided that would mean six pupils and three staff, the staff would be her, Tom Hicks and a.n.other depending on the volunteers if there were four females and two males the other staff member would be female or vice versa. Aileen waited an opportune moment before tackling Mike Smythe about the Mini Bus, she needn't have been so apprehensive, when she asked he replied, "There would be no problem he was just sorry he couldn't accompany them, all he needed was the drivers details and a list of people involved".

At the Ramblers Club meeting that evening the plans were revealed and a request for names of people interested in going, it was pointed out that there were only six places available, leave names with the secretary on the way out and they would have forty eight hours to finalise the list, Aileen was inundated with questions i.e. what was the cost what would they need to take with them etc?. Calum was asked if he had anything to add he said, "Yes it would be best if they took two rucksacks or at least one and a week-end bag,they would put their second week's clothes etc in the bag, they could leave that in the Mini Bus no point in carrying two weeks supply, in their own intrest they should travel as lightly as possible as it was a pretty strenuous hike". The young ones were really excited and wanted their names down as soon as possible but it was pointed out they would need parents permission.

As was usual Tom Hicks had to flex his muscles in his capacity as Chairman of the Ramblers club, he was unhappy about Calum's girl friend taking up a seat, he was quickly pulled to one side and in no uncertain terms it was pointed out that Calum was driving the bus there and back at no extra charge, after humming and hawing for a wee while it sunk in that he was best to keep his trap shut. The following day the kids started to bring written permission allowing them to put their names forward, there were far too many volunteers, the difficult part was eliminating kids without hurting their feeling, there were sixteen names, only six places available so it was unanimously agreed that the names would be put in a hat and a draw would take place.

The six lucky participants were duly chosen with the impriviso that when the next trip was due that this six would be the last to be included, this arrangement seemed to satisfy everybody, the split of the sexes were three of each a coin was tossed to determine if the third staff member would be male or female, Aileen was quite pleased to see it was a male she was a bit concerned about Tom Hicks being fit enough to tackle the two weeks ahead of them, the pupils were multi national with two West Indians, One Filipino, One Chinese and two Londoners.

The party left London on the Thursday evening, as Calum had suggested they each had two bags one for the first part of the hike and one for the second week. They arrived in Glasgow nine hours later in the early hours of Friday morning, they decided to find a place where they could have a good wash and then a decent breafast probably their last for a week, the teenagers were eager to get going, none of them had experienced the wild rugged Scottish countryside before. Calum was certain they would never be able to complete the whole hike in one week so he suggested that they should drive to Crianlarach and start off from there, it was only forty eight miles they should walk that in a week quite comfortably he would pick them up in Ft Willian on the Friday and take them to his mother's house where they could pitch their tent's and rest until Monday morning, the unanimous decision was to take Calum's advice. They arrived at Crianlarich just before lunch time, they had lunch and then started their hike, Calum left them but gave them his mother's phone number just incase of difficulties.

It didn't take the kids long to realise that the West Highland Way wasn't paved like the streets in their home borough of Bermondsey, soon they were beginning to feel the pace. Old Tom Hicks was proving to be a bit of a drawback, he was soon complaining about his knee joints and of course was soon lagging behind. Aileen let out a sigh and immediately Calums words sprung to mind, they were that the old fellow would struggle, they kept hiking until four pm, they had only covered about three miles but it was obvious that some of them were beginning to show some stress, Aileen called a halt, they found an area where they could camp for the night, their first day wasn't very fruitfull, by the time they had cooked some food and eaten, the midgies were beginning to bite, another hazzard none of them had experienced before.

Day two and Aileen was rather disappointed, she had asked that everybody be ready to start walking at eight thirty, her sights were set on hiking at least ten possibly twelve miles that day. It was nearing half past nine and the kids were still trying to pack their gear getting them out of bed was a nightmare especially the two West Indian girls. Ten minutes to ten and they were ready to go,

Tom Hicks was whinging with-in ten minutes his knees were sore walking on the uneven ground, some example he was to the teenagers. They stopped for some lunch at twelve thirty and Aileen reconed they had covered just over three miles so ten miles for the day was with-in their reach. They kept going until three pm and stopped for a twenty minute break Hick's list of complaints was getting longer every mile they walked until Aileen asked if he wanted to phone Calum to come and get him, but no he was quite content to keep going as long as he could moan and groan every step of the way, the kids had settled down and were beginning to enjoy the adventure, especially the scenery around Glencoe it was breath taking. On the Friday Aileen managed to get them on the road early they had stayed overnight in Kinlochleven so they had quite a hike to reach Ft William in reasonable time. Aileen checked the map it said sixteen miles she gathered their small group around her and gave them an insight of to-days hike, they were on the path at eight forty five she pointed out if they manged two miles an hour they would reach Ft Willam around four-o-clock so it was up to them,Calum would pick them up and drive them to where they could camp for the week-end. It was hard going but with a ten minute break every hour or so the miles soon began to disappear.

At five thirty the out skirts of Ft William were in sight, they had done very well and were getting better as they aclimatised to the conditions, of course Aileen was full of praise, the ever effervescent blonde bubbling over with enthusisiam. Calum was waiting for them, as usual Tom Hicks was like the cows tail, always at the rear he did a power of moaning but he wasn't that far behind and allowing for his sixty three years he was doing ok. They were all crowding round the mini bus, Calum was waiting until everybody was there so that they could hear what he had to say, "Did you all enjoy your hike?" with one voice they shouted "Yes". "Right load your gear into the bus and I will tell you what happens next" Once they were all seated in the bus Calum turned round and started to speak, "As most of you are aware my mother lives here, we were going to get you booked into a camping site but my kind hearted mam has said you can camp on her drying green and use her toilet facilities(it may be cramped).

She has a meal ready for everybody to-nite how does that suit you all", there was a round of applause, the kids had been looking forward to a Macdonalds or KFC. Instead they would have to do with mince and tatties followed by clootie dumplin and custard none of them had tried this Scottish Cuisine before.

Calum's Mam Nettie was over the moon, since his father died and his sister and him had left home she didn't really get a chance to cook for so many people, most evenings she would be on her own so she was in her element feeding a dozen hungry mouths, there was a rush for the bathroom, Calum laid down the law and said each person was allowed ten minutes in the shower so that everybody could have a turn. The next two days were free time they could do as they pleased, Calum told them that there was Highland Games in a little Glen called Glen Gair he intended going there as he had relatives who would be attending, it was always a chance to catch up, most of the young ones wanted to go with him. Tom Hicks wanted to go on the Steam Train to Mallaig so along with Jim Scott his fellow teacher they opted for that, a couple of the younger ones wanted to climb Ben Nevis but Calum wasn't keen on them going alone so he suggested they would go on Sunday as a party.

The drive from Corpach to Glen Gair, for Aileen was simply breath taking, the Commando Memorial at Spean Bridge was out of this world, the more Aileen saw of the Highlands the more she was falling in love with the place. Loch Lochy with its shroud of conifer trees was magnificent, the whole place was so clean and healthy looking, then there was the peace and quiet the complete opposite to Bermondsy. When they left the main road to drive up through Glen Gair village Aileen could not take in the beauty of the place, lovely old cottages on one side of the road with nearly a canopy of trees hanging over them, half way along the trees disappeared from one side and a Council Housing Scheme appeared, for the next half mile or so you had ancient one side and modern the other this didn't look out of place.

Calum had to explain what Shinty was, the sign on the gate welcomed you to Glen Gair Shinty Field and Heritage Centre they turned into the drive and were quite surprised to see an Arena with seats round the outside in the middle a full Pipe Band was playing. The games were amateur so admission was free but you could make a donation towards the upkeep of the facility, they were given a programme with the afternoon events, the last item on the agenda was the hill race five miles long, it stated that all entries were welcome. The London kids had never heard of a Hill race before so they were keen to enter. Calum said he would look for his cousin Hector he would keep them right, Hector was one of the few native Glen Gair dwellers, he was the grandson of Donald Macleod and the relationship between Calum and him was that their grandmothers were sisters. Hector was busy at the wheel of fortune one of the many fund raisers in the field, when he spotted Calum he called on his partner to take over while the two of them chatted, Calum asked about the young ones entering the Hill race and was assured they would be most welcome just line up with the rest at four o'clock the time the race started. Aileen had taken a ring side seat while Calum was sorting out the Hill racers, she was truly hooked with the place and started in motion the idea of selling up in London and moving to this area.

She asked Calum what his cousin did for a living, when told he was a joiner involved in building new houses and renovating Old Property she was most interested and wondered if she could have a chat with Hector. She would try picking his brains regarding the property situation in the area, she had a plan in mind but would keep it to herself in case she was gazzumpt.

The competitors were lined up for the hill race, they would be gone for about an hour so Aileen grabbed her opportunity to have words with Hector, he told her there were quite a few derelict properties on the market his choice would be the old Forestry Commision Stables, they were built by the Forestry just before the war so they were of sound structure, all the services were available, he said he would get Aileen an address where she could make enquiries, Hector asked what she had in mind if she got the property, she hedged her answer this was due to a story she had heard about the crafty Highlanders.

When the video rental boom hit the country this rather overweight Englishman decided to buy a van stock it with the latest videos, move to the Highlands where he would rent them out to the local villagers, his name was Cyril so the Highlanders immediately christened him Cyril Beag (Big Cyril) he started his round in the Ullapool/ Gairloch area, he sent out flyers letting the locals know what was going on and the day he would be in the village.

On his first day he visited ten villages and was most disappointed when he only managed to rent out ten videos, he put it down to the ignorance of the teuchters, but was sure when word got round business would improve. But no it was the same the next month one video in each village. What was really bugging him was that some of his tapes were worn done by the time he got them back they must have been played continually. His business didn't last too long when he discovered that the one video rented in each village was passed round the whole place and every villager had viewed it by the time Cyril Beag returned he found out the teuchters weren't so dim after all.

The Londoners had had a field day at the Glen Gair games the Hill Run participants were still rubbing their stiff muscles when the arrived back at Corpach. The unanimous decision for the evening was to go into town for their supper Aileen and Tom Hicks had invited Calums mother to join them, so there was a mad rush to get buckets and basins of hot water to wash and brush up before heading for the town. The Teenagers were still badgering Calum to take them up Ben Nevis on the Sunday, he pointed out that it was a very strenuous climb and in view of their early start to walk the Great Glen Way they should try something less taxing so he suggested that they take the Ski Lift at Anochmor, this would take them half way up the mountain and was less stressful,it was agreed they would take this option.

THE GREAT GLEN WAY

On the Sunday as promised Calum drove the party to Annoch Mor where they spent the afternoon in a very relaxed atmosphere, they were home early and started to pack the mini bus with the gear they would not require over the next week, it was stowed in a way that it wouldn't be touched again until they were back in London.It had been decided that Tom Hicks would drive the mini bus during the week, they weren't allowed to camp on the The Great Glen Route so at the end of each day they had to find a camping area to spend the night. Tom had volunteered to do the driving the idea being that he would drop them at the start of each section, then pick them up at the end of their day, while they were hiking he would find a camp site and set up the tents.

Monday morning was next to chaos as everybody tried to use the bathroom, get some breakfast and pack up their gear but it was a great team effort and they were ready to roll by eight thirty. As they had seen quite a bit of Ft William over the week-end it was decided to start the hike at Gairlochy, Neptune's Stair Case this would cut ten miles off the journey. When they arrived at the Lock Gates there was gasps of amazement the youngsters had never seen anything like it, this wonderful feat of engineering, if you looked to your right there was a magnificent view of Ben Nevis overlooking the whole scene. They said there goodbyes to Tom Hicks shouting see you to-night, the weather was beautiful and the scenery was mind boggling.

Aileen set off at a fair pace knowing that the farther they got when everybody was fresh the easier it would be later on when tiredness started to creep in, their target for the day was ten to twelve miles and it was achievable as the pathway was smooth and flat. As she tramped along her mind was working on what type of place she would like to set her roots down, an area where she could make a comfortable living, along the canal the oppertunities were never ending. Sailing, water skiing, fishing, walking, climbing it was real exciting stuff as opposed to what she had to endure in London. To be mugged, raped, murdered were all strong possiblities if you dropped your guard, even going to a cash machine was becoming an ordeal there were so many traps you could fall into and getting worse all the time, Aileen had made up her mind she was getting out, in the near future.

By the second day of their hike they had covered twenty five miles, Old Tom had found a camping area not far from Glen Gair, this had set Aileen's adrenalin going, she would try and get Tom to drive her over to the Glen in the evening so that she could have a look at the stables Hamish Macleod had talked about. She remembered from one of the tourist brochures that there was a Hydro Dam in Glen Gair with a Fish ladder where you could view the Salmon swimming up to get to the Dam, then on to their spawning grounds, she was sure the youngsters would appreciate that as many of them had never seen a live Salmon, herself included, she broached the subject with the Old fellow and for once in his life he was agreeable, they asked the kids if they would be interested, they got a one hundred percent response. As they passed the Shinty Field Aileen was really focused as she was sure Hamish had told her the stables were at the next turn off after the Cemetery.

Old Tom was no Lewis Hamilton, he crawled along at a very irritatingly slow pace, his passangers were delighted he wouldn't be driving back to London. But Aileen was quite thankful of his speed that evening it meant she could keep an eye out for the side road she was looking for, as they rounded the next bend she asked Old Tom to pull in and stop, she was at the right place as there was a for sale sign hammered into the grass verge. She made the pretence that the kids could view the river from the small bridge, her main goal was to give the derelict stables the once over, she wasn't disappointed the setting was a mind boggling scene, just like you would see on a post card or a calander. Aileen had her camera with her and proceeded to take at least a dozen pictures, she then photographed the forsale sign on the way back to the mini bus, her mission full filled the party headed for the dam and were quite disappointed to find the acess to the fish ladder locked and out of bounds, the young ones spent about twenty minutes taking photo's of each other to show the folks back home.

Back in the campsite Aileen, Tom Hicks and Hugh the third member of staff got out the intinery of the Great Glen Walk and summed up how far they had travelled in the past couple of days, they were quite pleased with their progress but didn't think they could cover the complete distance before Saturday, they would keep plodding on until Thursday evening and then weigh up the situation once again. They intended to arrive in Inverness on Saturday afternoon, get cleaned up, have some food, do some sightseeing, then get a few hours rest. After Tom Hicks had dropped them off on the final leg of their journey he would drive to Inverness, make arrangement with the campsite at the Bucht Park for them to Pitch their tents and use the washing up facilities, he would then drive to Ft William to meet up with Calum and Annie. They would leave Ft William at ten pm drive to Inverness pick the party up from the campsite, then at around mid-night they would start the journey back to London.

Late Friday afternoon the party started to arrive at Lewiston in dribs and drabs they had covered the fifteen miles from Invermoriston in eleven hours but they were feeling the stress it appeared the nearer they got to Inveness the more difficult the path got, this was about the most gruelling part of the journey they had encountered since they started. Once they were all aboard the mini bus Old Tom drove them to their campsite for the night, there were a few irritating midgies about but they had managed nearly two weeks without rain so that was a blessing, after some food the three teachers decidede to have a short meeting to discuss the last leg of their journey according to their map they still had nineteen miles to go and the terrain was similar as to what they had encountered to-day so it was agreed that they would never cover that distance in one day. Aileen wanted them to be in Inverness around two pm so that they could get a bit of rest and maybe the girls would want to do some shopping as there had been little opportunity along the route. Between the three teachers they decided to drive to the Blackfold Turn Off and start the remainder of their hike from there a distance of around eight miles it was put to the pupils who unanimously agreed with the proposal.

It had just turned eight thirty when the party piled into the mini bus for the final leg of their journey, the weather was kind to them, they were all in high spirits as they laughed and joked their way along the final leg of their journey.

The last eight miles were relatively easy and they arrived at the Canal Bridge just on one pm, at the campsite they were soon taking over the washing facilities, it was over a week since they had a real opportunity to wash away the grime from their week of hiking. The females in the party were soon ready and asking instructions on how to get to the city centre their first port of call was a resturant where they could buy a decent meal.

It was just on eleven pm when Calum drove into the campsite the party were all packed and ready to load up, half eleven and they were ready to roll, ten hours later they were hoping to be back home in London. The first hour of the journey passed in high spirits with many songs being sung,but tiredness soon over came the hikers and soon one by one they were dropping off to sleep.

The journey soon passed and just on nine am they were passing through the gates of their Bermondsey School after a bit of hand shaking and hugging they dispersed to their various homes it had been a wonderful adventure.

Aileen was quite tired so she shared a taxi with Old Tom they still had ten days before the holidays were over time to re-charge the batteries. She could hardly push the door of the flat open with the pile of mail behind it, the place smelt stale after two weeks of lying empty so she pushed the windows wide open and then put the kettle on. While the kettle was boiling she picked up her two weeks mail and sorted it into three bundles, junk mail/ begging letters, education correspondence and finally personal mail. She got quite excited with the the second one she picked up and noticed it was post marked Shetland Islands it could only be from Katie Foubister the friend she met in Glasgow. Katie was coming to London could Aileen meet up with her for a meal, she added she would have to behave herself as she was along with three colleagues, they had a party of twenty five school bairns to look after, she would reply later the next day, the answer would be yes, just let her know when they were arriving.

Back at school and Aileen was feeling quite depressed, her mind was made up she was moving to Scotland and it would be around the area she had just visited a few weeks ago, teaching was getting stale, mostly down to lack of disipline and human rights, teachers were actually afraid to leave themselves exposed, they were now liable to procecution for the most trivial of incidents and the kids knew how to play the system. Aileen had made up her mind, she intended getting in touch with the Forestry Commision Selling agents with regards to purchasing the derelict stables in Glen Gair she would send an e.mail asking for the details. She had been left some money by her parents when they passed away so with that and what she would get for her flat she was quite confident she would manage.

An answer by e.mail was waiting for her when she arrived home, in it she was told they would post on the itinery regarding the Stables which included about an acre of ground, sounded ideal and fitted Aileens plans just perfect. She decided to log on to the Highland Region Education Web Site in the off chance that they may have had teaching vacancies, her adrenalin gave a bit of a surge when she homed in on an advert looking for a relief teacher for the Lochaber Area it sounded perfect for her, she needed to be qualified to teach pupils as far as their fifth year, she needed transport and be available to stay away from home if the need arose.

Most importantly she needed to be available at a moments notice in the event of an emergency, one tasty line in the advert was that should she not be required she would be paid a generous retainer, wow if she could land this job she would have cracked it. Aileen wasted no time and e.mailed her C.V. there and then at the same time requesting an application form, things were happening so fast she was in danger of becoming overwhelmed, one dark cloud on the horizon was that her friend Calum had decided to leave the school and go back to his trade he also moved in with girl friend Annie, a bit of a blow for the school.

It took about five days for the Royal Mail to deliver the package regarding the Stables, Aileen was really keen on the place an item that caught her eye added by the selling agent was that should the site be developed and a boost to the tourist industry a grant may be available to help with the development, wow it was getting better all the time the asking price twenty thousand pounds. Aileen had to do some sums to see if her budget would stretch that far, she was still juggling figures about a week later when she received a repley to her application as a relief teacher and felt rather flattered that she was invited to attend an interview in Inverness at a time to be arranged, she would be advised on the date and time with-in the next three days but would get a week's advance warning, she was ecstatic, while in Inverness she could look further into the purchase of the Glen Gair stables, things were looking in her favour, she had also been told there would be a re-imbursement of expences.

In the mean time she received word from Katie Foubister she would be in London for five days, would Aileen be available to have a meal with her on the Wednesday evening, Aileeen checked the dates it was about six weeks away so yes she would make herself available, she e.mailed her friend and said they could get in touch nearer the date. By the end of the following week Aileen had received word back from the Education Authorities stating that they had arranged an interviw at eleven am on the Thursday morning would she confirm that this was suitable, Aileen e.mailed back that evening saying yes that arrangement would be fine. She decided to go by sleeper, leave London at nine pm arrive in Inverness early morning she would have all the facilities at hand so she could leave the train ready for her interview. After an uneventful journey the train arrived on time, Aileen had two hours before her interview so she decided to visit the selling agents office she asked a porter how far it was to Church Street and was told about a five minutes walk, that suited her fine,she booked her small overnight case into the left luggage, this would leave her with only her handbag and breifcase to carry. The young lady in the Agency office couldn't have been more helpful even offering Aileen a cup of coffee, she was already on file due to her email correspondance. They had a good chat and she was given a list of defunct Forestry commision property, she

explained that she had an interview for a job and if she was accepted she
would definitely be submitting an offer for the Glen Gair stables, an hour
later she was heading for the shopping centre for a browse round as she
passed the time. At twenty to eleven Aileen was heading for the Education
Offices the adrenalin was starting to pump, if she was successful this would
be her biggest career move to date.

There were three people behind the huge wooden table two women
one man, he was the oldest of the three, half-moon glasses and a green bow
tie with white spots.

They welcomed Aileen and told her to be seated then introduced
themselves he was head of Education for the Highlands and Islands the
younger woman was personel and the older woman was assistant to the
man, Aileen's head was in turmoil as she tried to grasp the names and
positions. The man cleared his throat and started off by telling Aileen
he was very impressed with her C.V, he then added that he thought the
position she had applied for was way below her qualifications, he thought
she should be aiming much higher. She answered by saying she had been
in the front line of teaching since she left teacher Training College and
had decided the time was right to have a career change which she hoped
would be much less stressful, she pointed out that teaching in London
had become a difficult job, then you had the stress of just living there it
was with you night and day, she went on to tell them of her two weeks
hiking from Glasgow to Inverness and how she had fallen in love with the
scenery and fresh air also the wide open spaces, a move to the Highlands
was her aim. Aileen endured well over an hour of interrogation, the
Education Chiefs knew their job and left no stone unturned, when they
announced that they were finished with her she looked at her watch and
noted it was still only twelve thirty she would have time on her hands,
she was asked if she could call back around four pm then she would get
an up date on what was happening. There was a spring in her step as she
left the office and headed back into town wondering what she would do
to pass the time till four-o-clock, she found her answer on the side of a

sightseeing bus, they were advertising trips to Cullodon Battlefield that sounded just perfect.

After a coffee in the bus station café Aileen boarded the open top bus heading for Cullodon Battlefield, she was amazed at how quickly you went from a built up area to open countryside ,in London you could drive for hours before you arrived in open country, then there was the traffic lights in London about a hundred yards between each set, traffic built up at every set of lights belching smoke fumes and dust into the atmosphere, health alone was a good reason to get out of London. She settled down to appreciate the scenery, she quickly noted how the landscape had changed completely from what it was between Glasgow and Inverness but the view to-wards Ben Wyvis was just as breathtaking, half an hour after leaving the city she was joining her fellow passengers reading the history of the Battle of Cullodon, after an intresting hour and yet another cup of coffee she was boarding the bus for the return journey, she arrived back in the city about half-past three nice time to make her way back to the Education Offices, she declined a cup of coffee from the receptionist thinking it would look bad if she had to ask the head of Education if she could leave the room. She had another adrenalin rush as she was called for another face to face, she was told to be seated bye the deputy head while the head cleared his throat. "Miss Grimshaw having spent over two hours debating the out come of our interviews it is always hard to tell people they have been unsuccessful", Aileen's jaw dropped about a foot but she soon perked up when Hugh Mackay continued, "But it gives me great pleasure when I tell the successful applicant the position is theirs", he waited for Aileen's response. She was totally gob smacked, at the back of her mind she had thought that she had very little chance especially as she was English, she finally managed to utter, "Thank You very much".

She then went through quite an emotional few seconds before she pulled herself together and listened to what Hugh Mackay had to say, "Miss Grimshaw you were in a short leet of three, it was a difficult decision to arrive at, but your experience as Assistant Head teacher gives us quite a bit of scope, many of our schools have one teacher, she has to carry out all the functions required of a teacher and head teacher so this is in your favour, also the fact that you have no small children to be taken into cosideration". He stood up and held out his hand "Welcome aboard the Highlands and Islands Education Authority", he went on to tell Aileen to speak with the personel lady and she would explain how things would swing into action.

Aileen tendered her resignation on returning to London she was to take up her new post in the Highlands in three months time, she had a lot of arrangements to make selling the flat etc, she also put in an offer for the Glen Gair Stables, so it was fingers crossed all round. She contacted her friend Katie and they arranged to meet for a meal, it was a laugh a minute but Katie was in her professional role as Head Teacher responsible for twenty five teenagers and four adult staff so there was no drinking or gambling she was on her best behaviour, she made a pact with Aileen that when she was settled in her new role they would meet up in Aberdeen and paint the town red one week-end.

It was all systems go in London Aileen's boss was most disappointed that she was leaving, he had earmarked her to take over when he retired in just over a year's time, but deep down he was in total agreement with her move, London was a pure rat race, at least one Head Teacher had been murdered recently, how were you supposed to teach pupils when lots of them were unteachable, yes if he had been Aileen's age he would also be looking at moving to pastures new.

The date given for Aileen to start work in her new job was the twenty eigth of May, she sat most evenings trying to come up with an idea of what she would do for a place to stay, discussing it with her friend Tom Hicks one evening he came up with the idea of why not buy a camper van, immediately Aileen thought what a wonderful idea at least she would have some where to sleep at night until she had sorted things out. She went round a couple of garages next day and managed to get a van at a reasonable price but did note that they were quite expensive.

Aileen had tidied up all the loose ends of her move from London to the Scottish Highlands, in the second week in May she set forth for the long journey North, she had decided to drive as far as the borders and stay overnight, the next day she would head for Inverness, she had an appointment with the selling agents who were carrying out the transactions for the Glen Gair Stables. She arrived in the Highland Capital late in the afternoon and decided to book in to the Municipal Caravan Park at the Bucht Park, her appointment was next morning. Her meeting with the agency was quite fruitful, she was given the good news that her offer of just over Twenty thousand pounds had been accepted, this was brilliant news everything was going to plan, after clearing up the paper work she was free to go and inspect her Highland Retreat, she was hoping to reside on the site but that may prove difficult until she had all the services restored according to the title deeds everything including sanitation was waiting to be connected.

She arrived mid afternoon and had a look round a slight shudder ran down her spine as she wondered if she had made the right move in buying the site, but it was a bit late to worry now, in for a penny in for a pound.

Turning the clock back fifty years on hearing that a Londoner had purchased the Forestry Stables old Alex Dubh would have shaken his head and muttered "Another White Settler yea yea," even though his daughter had married a Londoner anybody who wasn't a native Glen Gairian was regarded as an intruder in Old Alex's eyes. Little did he know that if the White Settlers stopped coming the Glen would be an empty wilderness, gone were the days when there was an abundance of work available on the door step ,those days were in the past along with a big proportion of the younger generations of Glen folks who had moved in order to earn a living, of the originals very few resided in the Glen.

The main family in the Glen before and after World War 2 were the Mellis's Col Mellis was the Laird and Master he had three of a family, they left home at the outbreak of war and never returned finding highly paid jobs in the city after their war service, much easier than struggling to

keep a Highland Estate on a profitable footing. The War also disrupted
the sporting side of the estate the most profitable side. Then when old Col
Mellis died death duties killed off the estate for good, it was broken up
and sold to various projects interested in aquiring ground, Hydro, Forestry
etc. All that remained of the Mellis empire was a small area of ground on
which a modern bungalow had been built the owner was a grand daughter
of Col Mellis she was getting on in years and employed a handyman to
look after her ponies and keep the place tidy. All the little cottages which
had once belonged to the Estate were now privately owned and many had
huge extensions built at the back in many cases this spoiled the shape of
the old houses but they were under a preservation order and the front and
original shell could not be altered. One of the old brigade and part of the
back bone of the Glen was Donald Macleod, Donald preached the gospel
until he was no longer able. Out of his family of four none of them reside
in the Glen his only resident relative is his grandson a time served joiner
who lives with his partner Seonaid Maceanruig in a council house, he is
one of the few residents who works from Glen Gair and travels home every
night, his partner is also off an old established family, her uncles were the
MacLennan brothers Chaps and Buckshot she has a family of four and is
quite unique in the fact that three of her four siblings live in the village. Alex
Dubh passed away over twenty years ago, his son still resides in the village
and like his father did, he works for the Council Roads Agency. Dan Fraser
built up his business, this is now run by his son and daughter-in-law they
have mini buses and hire cars. Old Archie Cormack died rather young due
to an accident, he had six of a family but sadly they are all gone except for
one although there are a few grand children still resident in the village. But
the school role reflects on the amout of child bearing couples still living in
the village, there are only twenty pupils attending the local primary school
it could be in danger of being closed down in the near future if the children
attending declines any further.

The main hub of the village in bygone days was the Hotel with its
pub built away from the main building so that the local drunks would not
disturb the paying guests.

Friday and Saturday evenings would see the wooden bar bursting at the seems as the men of the village would dispense of their hard earned cash, a whisky and a half pint would cost about half-a-crown twelve and a half pence in decimal currency, there were eight half crowns to the pound so it was possible to get smashed for one pound bearing in mind the wages were approx five pounds a week that would be a fifth of the wages spent in the pub in many cases this was before they had been home on pay day, but bear in mind the liscencing laws were very tight, the hours were five pm until nine pm in the winter and five pm until nine thirty pm in the summer, not very long if you wanted a decent fill before chucking out time.

The Hotel now belonged to yet another family of white settlers, they no longer opened the Hotel side of the business in the winter, only the bar and the Resturant but its changed days in the bar, they may only have half-a-dozen clients and very rarely is it bursting at the seams, of course a whisky and a half pint will now cost you in the region of four pounds so people cant afford many nights out with the modern day costs.

Aileen Grimshaw the latest White Settler to boost the flagging population of Glen Gair had arrived, she had a massive task ahead of her. Firstly she had to find a place to stay, her camper van was fine for a couple of nights but she needed a permenant base. She still had about ten days before she started work, this was a two week course in Inverness College, so that she could go through the systems used by the Highland Education Authority. She decided to book into a bed and breakfast for the two weeks, driving back to Glen Gair for the week-end. During her first visit to the city she did some detective work as she tried to procure funding for her project at the Stables. Her first move would be to find a reasonably priced Architect whom she would get to draw up plans, this done she would then need to get planning permission, she had her work cut out if she was to be up and running for the following spring. To save her a big outlay of finance she decidede to buy a thirty foot mobile home and stand it on her property near the stables, she was allowed to do this as it could be classed as a site office, it would be quite easy to get the services connected that would be a big step forward.

Aileen settled into GlenGair and loved the place,she was lucky in as much as she had a steady job all be it she had to travel to some rather remote areas, it was all a new experience. In between times she was chasing people trying to get her project moving. She started to get quite frustrated when she come up against red tape, first it was the planning people they were never in a hurry worse still they only convened once in a while, the waiting was getting to her. She had one outlet when the going got tough, she would return to Glen Gair on the Friday afternoon pack her hiking gear in her Volkswagen Campervan, then head into the wilderness and chill out with a day of hiking she would then find a place to park up on the Saturday evening hopefully near a pub where she could relax over a couple of beers. It was amazing the amout of friends she made during these very relaxing hiking sorties. She was eventually granted planning permission, this allowed her to make enquiries about raising the finances, again red tape, frustration was the order of the day, but she was desperate to find financial help otherwise she would have to go into heavy debt, this was a very expensive alternative.

The New Glen Gair Village Hall catered for quite a few events over the year, because of the overdraught needed for the construction of the building it was imperative that as many events as possible should be held, there were all sorts of different persuits. In the summer of that year Glen Gair Village Hall hosted a rather unique event in the form of a Diamond Wedding Anniversary Party. It was unique in two or three different ways. One person went into W.H.Smith the news agents looking for a sixtieth wedding anniversary card he was rather taken aback when there were only two on display. He asked the assistant if that was all they had available, "Yes there's not a lot of need for many more now-a-days" she replied, "half the population don't bother to get married, over half of the half that do, get divorced, then there's natural wastage so to reach the Diamond Anniversary stage in modern times is quite an achievement."

Lizzie and Shamus were the unique couple, they had reached sixty years of married bliss. They no longer lived in Glen Gair having retired to another of the Great Glen villages quite some time ago, infact none of the family lived in Glen Gair. Lizzie was more or less a native although she liked people to know that she was born and part raised in a Glasgow Tenement having moved to the Glen at an early age. Shamus was native to the village they now lived in during their retirment. He had spent many years working and living in Glen Gair until modern technology swallowed up the jobs with the Hydro Board and they had to move. The party had been organised by their married daughter and daughter-in-law, the invitations were sent out to friends and relations the final tally being around eighty. Quite a few of the original Glen families were represented, they had travelled from their homes to be present at this unique occasion, looking round the assembled guests many were elderly, well into their seventies. Lizzie and Shamus at the top table were surrounded by their immediate family of grand children and great grandchildren. Their only daughter and their daughter-in-law did a marvellous job keeping things organised, the ladies who served the food from the excellent buffet have also to be mentioned for their efficient handling of their part of the proceedings. It was a grand evening and as well as a Diamond Wedding Party many of the older natives of Glen Gair met up for the first time in many years, some of them had attended school together and were well over seventy years of age, they had time to re-new aquaintances. Unfortunatly like all good things the party had to come to an end and the older people started to drift off home to their adopted residences but it was good to have a Ceilidh and meet up with old friends.

THE WHITE SETTLERS

Many of the Highland Glens are now typical to Glen Gair, very few of the residents are native to the Glen they live in, as I said previously the younger generations had to move to the big towns and cities to find employment. Many of the Local Authority Houses in the Glens are owned by the Council or their represantitive agencies, this means that if a house becomes vacant the Agencies have only one thought in mind that is to get it occupied as soon as possible so that they don't miss out on rent, hence a contributing factor to the demise of the local Glen natives, as long as there are bums on seats the Housing Agencies are not too fussy if they are natives or not.

In the early days when a new family appeared in the Glen the phrase White Settler was treated as a bit of a joke, one of the first to use the phrase in Glen Gair was none other than Alex Dubh. As time progressed and people in the affluent areas of England began to sell their houses at extortionate prices, they were looking to make a quick kill. Why not use the Highlands of Scotland to exploit the property market. Houses selling in England for half a million pounds would leave the owner with a handsome profit when he shelled out less than fifty thousand for a huge new house in a remote Highland Glen. In my mind there were three categories of White Settler, firstly there was the ones allocated Council Houses in many cases it would be a single parent or maybe a disabled elderly couple in both cases they would be living on benefits. The second category were the English ones who snapped up the small business's such as bed and breakfast establishments, they could sell their property in England for a Kings Ransom come to the Highlands and buy very cheaply, some as in the case of Aileen Grimshaw would have a go at starting up a brand new business. The down side about the ones in this category is that many of them were still young enough to work. Once the business was established one or other of the couple would run the business while the other went to work, this meant that they were filling a job that was maybe badly needed by the local population but that's life. The third category was the rent-a-mob crowd, they were filthy rich people, retired and prepared to pay a fortune for a secluded property preferably over looking a Loch. They had spent their life living in places like Brighton, Bournemouth, Kent or Sussex, they were the commuter brigade. Many of them spent three hours a day travelling to and from their luxurious pad to the City of London where there was continual overcrowding, where ever you went in London there was a continual flow of people on the pavements, on the streets there were an assortment of vehicles belching fumes into the atmosphere, if ever the term rat race could be used to describe a place it was a perfect name for London. The ones in this category were proper snobs they didn't participate in any of the activities in the Glen, kept them selves to themselves pottering about their palatial home. Who could blame them, life in the South Of England was becoming a nightmare, at the back of peoples minds was the thought of another Terrorist Attack, the fear of being assaulted.

Even to draw your own money from a hole-in-the-wall could also be a risky business, there was no pleasure in living in this enviroment. Their main outlook in life now was to guard their new found privacy and guard it they did.

But the rent-a-mob were not the quiet unassuming people that they were considered to be, as soon as any changes to the landscape was suggested they swung into action opposing every change that was mentioned. As soon as the new Pylon Line from Beauly to Denny was mentioned they swung into action protesting and doing their best to disrupt the plans. Another development they strongly opposed was the construction of Wind Farms again they tried to show their muscle every time a new site sought planning permission. These people were well off, they were able to afford the best money could buy but they didn't want anybody else to reap the benefits that they were used to, their patch of the Highlands was sacred.

All was not lost for Glen Gair and other Highland Glens with the craving for re-newable energy, every nook and cranny was being looked at in the hope that they could resurect the building of more Hydro Electrict Schemes. The labour force would need to start from scratch as all the old hands had passed on or maybe retired. But would the younger generation be interested in working in bleak outlandish work sites roughing it in work camps like their forefathers did, it would be intresting to see how it panned out.

In the mean time Aileen was finding out it was not all plain sailing in her quest for funding for her proposed project, she was very reluctant to get herself into debt. The banks were in turmoil as were the mortgage lenders so she was at a loss, she still had money in her bank account but not nearly enough for what she intended doing. She toyed with the idea of taking on a partner,the down side to this was that if they ever got off the ground she would need to earn double. She finally settled to put everything on hold until the following spring. She had an invite to go to Shetland for Christmas and the New Year Big Katie had kindly offered her a room, it turned out to be quite an adventure.

Aileen had the adventure of a lifetime crammed into one week in Shetland boy do these people know how to party, the one downside was the hassle to get there, Aileen had driven to Aberdeen and caught a flight, she didn't fancy a twelve hour sail on probably very rough seas but it had been worth it, one sure thing was that she would be back in the summer when she would get some walking and exploring, she was assured by Katie and her friends she would be welcome anytime, she left with a bag full of local produced goodies the likes she had never seen before.

One of Katie's neighbours who was also a good friend happened to be a high ranking official with the Shetland Tourist Board, Katie had told him about Aileens proposed project and the difficulty she was having with funding, Frank Peacock sat with her for an afternoon and tried to come up with a plan that may help but he did explain that at the minute money was very scarce all round. He asked Aileen what sort of obsticles she was coming up against, she wrote them all down. One was that she had never ran or managed a business before, two she had no experience of tourism, three the type of business she was trying to set up was untried before except in large outward bound establishments, four was that she had no assets apart from the site if the business were to fail, the list was endless.

Aileen arrived back in Glen Gair on the fifth of January she was badly in need of some rest keeping up with Katie and her friends was real strength sapping stuff, the locals must have been made of caste iron as they never seemed to need a lot of rest where as Aileen needed her eight hours per night, any deviation from this routine left her feeling shattered.

Her mobile home was like an ice box even although one of her neighbours had started the heating up, once she had the cooker going with some food and the wood burning stove going full blast it was soon nice and cosy she had turned off the water before she left incase of frozen pipes but the weather was surprisingly mild with very small traces of snow but no ice, unusual for a Scottish January.

She had her first taste of icy roads the day she returned to work, she had never experienced anything like it before, the experience left her rather wary of what lay ahead she had to drive forty miles each way. Going home late afternoon was no problem as the roads were all clear again, the morning escapade had left Aileen wondering if she would be better staying in B&B for the two weeks she would be working in that location, winter weather had never entered her original plans. One of the pieces of advice she had been given while in Shetland was to badger her local M.P, she didn't even know who he or she was but would start making enquiries, she had to confirm if she could go ahead with her project. There were ideas other than the one's from her original plans, ideas that were maybe cheaper, such as doing away with accommodation maybe purchasing a couple of caravans, also to set up pitches for tents, most hikers and bikers carried their own sleeping equipment, so the cheaper options were there but not quite what she had set out to achieve.

As time wore on Aileen began to realise her dream was fading fast, trying to borrow money at reasonable rates was near impossible, she thanked her lucky stars she had a job all be it you could say her jacket was on a shooglie nail. At the present time no job was safe the unemployment register was getting longer every week. The Vultures were moving in on Aileen that is men trying to buy her site at a cut price, although she hadn't made any progress with her holiday hostel she was still teaching and receiving a monthly wage packet so she was doing ok. The move from London to the Highlands including the purchase of the site had set her back thirty thousand pounds, local housing contractors were offering her less than Ten Thousand for her site a bit of an insult, if she had been desperate that would have been a different story.

WHERE DID IT ALL GO WRONG

Aileen Grimshaw is just a character in my story but I have evidence of young people trying to set up their own business and being knocked back when they tried to borrow a couple of thousand pounds. These people should be getting all the help possible to boost their moral and maybe the economy instead of meeting with a blank wall.

My favourite male film star was the great Jimmie Stewart he had a sort of magical way about him, in one film he was asked to describe himself, talking in the Western Drawl that only he could execute he said "I'm just a regular sort of guy I guess", well that's just how I would describe myself.

The following chapters are how I the Author saw the decline in our country, our standard of living and of course job opportunities for our younger generations. In my opinion it all went wrong with the discovery of Oil and Natural Gas on our door step in the North Sea. I lived through the War, the fifties, the sixties and into the seventies. People's standard of living, wages and opportunities had advanced in leaps and bounds nobody was really poor and there was always plenty work available.

There was great excitement when it was announced that Britain would be producing Oil & Gas by the middle Seventies. The final Hydro Electric Scheme was nearing completion in nineteen seventy three, it was constructed at Foyers above Loch Ness but due to the high costs of Construction there would be no more water powered production of Electricity. Think about this, the water that drives the Turbines is free supplied curtsy of God anybody can use it, so why the statement that it was too expensive. The building of the Power Stations had been ongoing for about twenty five years. I have no idea how many Hydro Schemes were built but as far as I am aware they were always built on time and with-in budget. If the Construction Company ran over their time and delivered late they would be heavily fined. The tools used to build the schemes were way behind what is available in modern times, a lot of work was carried out using pick's and shovel's, here is the bit that makes me proud of having been part of the Hydro Builders Workforce, I have never heard of any major failures on any of the Hydro Sites in the Highlands yes there would be breakdowns due to wear and tear but the workmanship was sound carried out by proud conscientious workers.

Nineteen seventy three saw the Oil Rig Construction industry take off the two main yards at Nigg and Arderseir ran training programmes building up a workforce of their own trained men, once they had passed the required tests they were paid the top rate of ninety pence per hour, there was no shortage of recruits with men moving from all over the country to get a job. The result of this was that the local building trade began to suffer as they lost many of their highly skilled tradesmen, joiners and brickies trained as fitters and welders at the Construction Yards. With-in months the car parks at the yards were filled with rows and rows of brand new cars many of them top of the range, on the housing front it was the same the money lenders were throwing money at the Oil Workers like it was going out of fashion. The standard of living had taken a mighty leap forward. Both yards suffered from a lengthy industrial dispute, this caused the money lenders a bit of a head ache because the men were more or less living from hand to mouth, getting no wages was a problem.

Because the men would have a week lying time and a weeks wages to lift at the end of the first week of the dispute they would more than likely be able to meet their commitments but the second month would be a different story. They would have to feed the family pay for heating and lighting leaving more or less no money to pay for the Mortgage and the Hire Purchase on the car, the first missed payment would warrant a reminder, the second month would probably be a red letter, if it went to a third month the law at the time was that the H.P company was supposed to reclaim the car. One H.P company I knew of had twenty six Oil Workers cars on their books the Manager had no idea what to do, his dilemma was solved just before the twelfth week when the strike was called off. Everything settled down and work was resumed, it was now nineteen seventy eight rumours were rife that there was no more orders on the books and mass redundancies were on the cards at both Highland Yards, like all good rumours this one also eventually came true, both yards made over one thousand men redundant, everybody received a payout, many of the guys volunteered to go just to receive the redundancy money, it would be a short term fix for many of them. This was to be the trend with the oil business boom and burst, into nineteen eighty and the Yards were back in full swing, they were like that until nineteen eighty nine when the next down turn occurred.

Into the nineteen eighties and the North Sea Natural Gas was almost ready to be used for domestic purposes. Before it could be used all the gas appliances in the British Isles had to have a modification carried out, this huge project was carried out by British Gas Engineers free of charge. There was a huge advertising campaign urging people to change to this new cheap wonder tool, so naturally people are always on the look out for a bargain, but after throwing away the dirty messy coal fire and possibly the oil fired central heating system did anybody stop to think that once you made the conversion to gas that was it, there was no turning back unless you were willing to pay massive costs to re-install your old system, we were now trapped by British Gas, I'm afraid the cheap gas only lasted for so long, we then found ourselves at the mercy of the six main players in the gas supply industry. Of course when we had plentiful supplies instead of looking to the future we sold our gas to all and sundry leaving ourselves short and at the mercy of the countries who sell natural gas, what used to be a pleasure is now a big worry.

In my opinion for what its worth I feel that Britain was on a slippery slope before the Tories lost power in nineteen ninety seven, the man to replace John Major was the most useless prime minister I can recall, by the time we were rid of him, Tony Blair I am talking about, he had us involved in a full scale war in Iraq then Afghanistan his reign was the start of the decline of our country, he was too busy lining his own pockets to see that others such as Bankers and Politicians were helping themselves to tax payers money also. The old people had a saying that if you took to much out of the well it will eventually run dry how true. Tony Blair lasted for ten years before the country finally got rid of him but the legacy of untold damage he left behind is really worrying. One particular incident that always bugs me is the death of Dr Kelly the expert on Iraq's Weapons of Mass Destruction, my heart goes out to his family whatever happened to him was uncalled for, what I could see of him he was an honest clever man who told the truth maybe that was his downfall.

After getting rid of Blair and his henchmen the job of Prime Minister was handed to Gordon Brown he had been waiting in the wings for the past couple of years, whilst carrying out the task of Chancellor, it was always thought that he was doing a brilliant job, but in the aftermath of the banking fiasco it is doubtful if he knew what was going on, his reign as P.M lasted until he was forced to resign in two thousand and ten, if our top men were so useless what chance had us lesser minions.?

During the thirteen years the Labour Government were in power the money they wasted on some of the most awful looking structures they approved and then funded to the tune of Millions of pounds. Before the Tories were booted out of power they had started moves to build the Millennium Dome it was just in the planning stage when Blair was elected as Prime Minister he didn't think the plans were grand enough or elaborate enough so he had it redesigned and made bigger no doubt most of the readers will remember the fiasco it turned out to be at a cost of seven hundred and eighty nine Million pounds, I am aware it is in England but it was funded with tax payers money. But we in Scotland haven't escaped the modern building fiasco, just look at our Scottish Parliament building an ongoing problem, the first being the cost, it was opened in nineteen ninety nine at a cost of four hundred and thirty one million pounds ten times over budget the mind boggles. The first major crisis was when a roof support beam suddenly broke loose and came crashing to the floor luckily nobody was maimed or killed, if this building was properly designed and the work inspected by a Clerk-of-Works on a regular basis how could this happen.? The last major expense associated with the Hollyrood White Elephant was having to get access to the ceiling in order to fit hanging scaffold brackets, I presume this was an oversight at the time of Construction so adding all the repairs and other expense how much did this modern building actually cost, doesn't bare thinking about.

It grieves me to see the shoddy workmanship that is accepted to-day, I am not talking about major projects but Private Houses, sold for anything over one hundred and eighty thousand pounds the faults I have heard about and witnessed is quite worrying especially when it comes to the Electric's in the house, gardens with no drainage and because of the buried rubble it is impossible to spike the lawn, it used to be when new houses were built all the black ground that had been moved to allow the building to be carried out, was then scattered around the house to a depth of possibly two feet this allowed the new owner to have a nice garden, this no longer happens, the rubble if raked flat and then covered with turf with the result that every time it rains the lawn is like a swamp until the atmosphere dries it up. Hope we never run short of vegetables as it will be impossible to grow them in our modern gardens.

Nearly every country worldwide has a transport system that includes trams even the very poor countries, Scotland used to have trams in Aberdeen, Edinburgh and Glasgow but in the fifties they were deemed to be redundant, the rails were removed and we then had the choice of buses or taxi's. Then in two thousand and eight it was decided by the Edinburgh Council that due to congestion, cost of fuel etc they would re-instate the Tram car system it was to be a straight forward system from the City Centre to the Airport it sounded like a good idea, the Contract was awarded to a German Company, supposedly experts at constructing a Tramway system.

Sadly there has been nothing but hassle from day one, the work had been on going for four years and its doubtful if its half way to being completed, they continually run out of money, stop work, then after costly delays its all systems go, the latest hand over date is twenty fourteen. When the first estimates were submitted in two thousand and three they were for three hundred and seventy five million pounds the latest estimates of the cost when completed will be around one billion pounds. How can the companies be so far out in their estimates, or maybe they don't care knowing that the government will have to cough up in order to get the work completed. The length of this tram journey is only eight point one miles the most costly tramway in the modern world.

The twentieth century ended and the brand new twenty first century was born, many millions of pounds were spent ushering the world into the New Millennium, the Dome in London being one of the costliest. Once the dust and celebrations had settled and the cold light of day was realised Two Thousand was not a happy time in the Highlands of Scotland the Oil Construction Yards were in their death throes there was no work, the little there was seemed to be going to foreign yards in Spain, Holland and even Korea, seemingly it was cheaper to go to the Far East build a Rig then tow it halfway around the world than what it was to build it in Scotland. But the end was positive when the Arderseir Yard closed, within a very short period of time it was wiped off the map. Nigg struggled on until the middle of July two thousand when the final Rig to be built in the Moray Firth was completed, The Elf Elgin sailed away to her final berth in August two thousand, Nigg never closed completely but in over ten years no major work has taken place. The Yard has just been bought over so you never no there may be a revival on the cards. Soon after the Oil Construction yards ceased to function the house building industry collapsed then the Banks started to go bankrupt due to the greedy dishonest people who were running them and sadly the Government.

We entered a period of mass unemployment thousands made redundant no body could afford to buy a house and many of the people who had bought at extortionate rates were now in dire straits because their houses were worth less than what they paid for them, this little episode landed people in a lot of debt.

If you think back, when the Foyers Hydro Scheme was completed the cry went out no more water driven Hydro plants they are far too expensive, well lo and behold in two thousand and three it was announced the Hydro Board had been given the go-ahead to build a brand new scheme, it would be the biggest in Britain and produce enough power to service a city the size of Glasgow. It was to be built at Glendoe near Ft Augustus above Loch Ness, I remember thinking good probably five hundred badly needed jobs. Right from the start it was kept rather secretive, low key, there would be a press announcement occasionally but nothing sensational. Then one day there was an announcement that a German Company Hochtief had been awarded the contract worth around one hundred and fifty Million Pounds, there was about fifteen Km of tunnel work but this was to be done using the machine that was used on the Channel Tunnel so no need for conventional Tunnel Tigers, everything was to be done by one huge boring machine, no doubt that would do away with a hundred or so jobs.

Still it was thirty years since the last scheme was Constructed, yes there would no doubt be many changes of equipment from the old days of the pick and shovel. As I said previously the Scheme at Glendoe was like a Clock and Dagger Operation, no publicity, then in the daily newspaper there was a column saying that Hochtief would be shipping their giant boring machine by road. As the vehicles were quite massive they would carry out the operation overnight on a Saturday so as to try and keep traffic disruption at a minimum, this was done and very little hassle was encountered. A few weeks later in a blaze of publicity our Prime Minister Tony Blair was all over the media cutting the first turf, hearlding the start of the Glendoe Hydro Electric scheme.

Although I am retired I still take a keen interest in what is happening on the work front. On a visit to the Fort Augustus area I happened to mention to a friend that the men of the Glen would be enjoying having work on their doorstep once again and having a job that allowed them to travel home every night. He looked at me as though I had a hole in my head and said. "There is not one local working on that scheme all the workers are Poles brought over especially for this job". I was flabbergasted to say the least, all the men and youths sitting at home drawing benefits, this could not be right, what got to me was the sneaky way they went about it there is not much wonder there was no publicity. Where the hell was the Member Of Parliament or even the Local councillors when this deal was done. I often wonder why it was done there were enough men on the dole to man up Glendoe a dozen times yet the Government allowed foreigners to take the work away from local Scots people. My feelings are that the Poles were paid a much lower rate than what the Scots would work for thus allowing Hochtief to submit a lower tender to get the work. The next blaze of publicity was a visit by the new Prime Minister Gordon Brown he detonated a small explosive charge in order to trigger off another Phase of the Scheme.

Then in the biggest blaze of Publicity it was announced that the Glendoe Hydro Scheme was complete and would be officially opened by Her Majesty The Queen on the twenty ninth of June two thousand and nine. It was a huge opening ceremony with many dignitaries arriving by chopper the media made a meal of it. The German Construction Company Hochtief were praised to the highest for the efficient way they carried out the work on time and with-in budget. I never ever heard any word of the four hundred Poles who were hired to do Scottish Jobs. During the Queens visit did the Poles sing God Save our Gracious Queen or maybe they had a sheet with the words for Flower Of Scotland who knows.

As far as I am aware Glendoe started to produce Electricity the minute the Queen pressed the start button. But Glendoe didn't have its troubles to seek because after three month of production everything ground to a halt, the roof of the main tunnel had collapsed disrupting the flow of water. It is not unusual to experience a fall of rock in an unlined tunnel but normally it could be cleared up quite quickly, unfortunately the Glendoe Rock fall must have been huge and possibly too dangerous to move, this resulted in a new smaller tunnel having to be built to by pass the rock fall. The cost of this operation thirty five million pounds there is an ongoing battle trying to ascertain blame and who will pick up the tab at the end of the day.

It is well known that the Great Glen sits on a Geographical Faultline making the rock very unstable, when the Foyers Scheme was built there were quite a few problems with falling rock how they overcame this I'm not sure, there are various methods of dealing with unstable rock. The finger must be pointed at the geologists who gave the go-ahead that the rock was safe to be mined, in my opinion some body was careless and didn't do a proper job, after the experience of Foyers you would think they would have been more vigilant. The fact that they used a boring machine as opposed to the conventional drilling machines and explosives probably didn't help because, I am sure, if they had used explosives the roof would have caved in long before it did, but as I said earlier everything was so hush, hush we may never know who is at fault. There is talk of future Hydro Electric Schemes being constructed I just hope that the SNP Government insist our Scottish work force are given the opportunity to get involved. The sad part is that we now have at least one generation of people who have never worked they don't know how to work because they have never had the opportunity, in many cases this is because there is only one parent in the family most likely the mother, she may never ever have had a job either because she started breeding soon after leaving school. Many of that Generation don't get out of their beds until near mid-day, you can tell them if you meet them on the street their hair is still wet from the shower.

Over the last few years many of our major projects have had Foreign input, Like Hollyrood, The Edinburgh Trams and then Glendoe in all these projects something has gone wrong, thus costing millions of pounds over budget. What we need to do is look around at what we Scots achieved without any foreign input. We built some of the biggest ships in the World on the Clyde Shipyards, never heard of many major problems, we built Hydro Electric Schemes all over Scotland until Glendoe never heard of any major mishaps, then more recently we built huge Oil Rigs costing Millions of pounds never heard of any major problems. Now if you are going anywhere near Edinburgh as you cross the Firth Of Forth have a look at the magnificent Forth Rail Bridge now looking resplendent in her newly painted coat, built by Scottish labour and opened one hundred and twenty two years ago. To achieve this mammoth task it took seven years at a cost in money of three million pounds, the human cost was fifty seven killed a high price in human lives. It would have been a dangerous place to work the weather would have been a major hazard, then the scaffolding probably quite hap hazard, on top of that the machinery as we know it to-day was not available so a lot of work would have been done by brute force and ignorance. If the same structure was to be built to-day what would it cost the mind boggles?.

We are now into the first month of twenty twelve and the doom and gloom continues, the Governments are squabbling about an independence referendum, what they should be doing is all pulling together to try and sort out the mess our country is in. Already the media are reporting companies closing down and mass redundancies, the unemployment figures are horrendous, then we keep hearing there are at least one million illegal immigrants in our Country, how do they survive.?

DISCIPLINE

In my humble opinion one word sums up many of the modern day problems, that word is discipline, or should I say, rather a lack of it. In my young day the first discipline you experienced was potty training, at roughly a year old your mother would start you off, if after a week you were still reneging she would administer the first discipline with a smack across the bum, nothing too serious unless you continued to throw tantrums. The next piece of training was table manners, father usually administered the discipline at the meal table, all meals were eaten in a civilised manner with the family sitting at the table in virtual silence, nobody left the table until the meal was finished. This was also when you were introduced to knowing how to work, well in our house anyhow the family took it in turns to wash and dry the dishes. I suppose the introduction of the dish washer killed off the need for the dishes to be hand washed. In many of the modern households of to-day nobody sits at the dining table, the plates are grabbed from the kitchen and the family lounge's on sofas, bean bags or whatever while watching the television, this also kills off the art of conversation.

The next phase of discipline training and showing respect started when you went to school. In my ten years of schooling I never heard one pupil back chatting the teacher, they were too well respected and were not adverse at dishing out punishment if it was required. Now the press are for ever reporting various misdemeanours that take place in our schools, then I often wonder about the quality of teachers we have, quite often we read reports of teachers committing sexual abuse on both male and female pupils, teachers suing the Education Authorities for huge sums of money because they suffered from stress, then you have instances of teachers being assaulted by unteachable pupils.

In Scotland according to the statistics there are fifty nine thousand households where there is either an alcohol or drug related parent, that's a lot of people, but just think if there are two children in each household being brought up in this environment that's potentially one hundred thousand deranged children joining the ranks in a few years time.

On leaving school most of my generation found jobs, this furthered your knowledge of discipline where you had to respect the elder members of the work force, step out of line and a clip round the ear would remind you to show respect. On reaching eighteen, depending on your employment you were called up for two years National Service. This was the final piece of the jigsaw where you were taught discipline, smartness and respect, when you left the services you were an independent man. Finally on being demobbed you would meet a young lady get married produce a family, it was then up to you to teach your kids how they should behave and grow into decent hard working citizens, I have always felt that your early training stayed with you all your life.

Another part of my life that I thought was essential towards discipline was having to attend Sunday School. Although I am ashamed to admit I don't attend Church although I always find the lessons very interesting on the odd occasions I do happen to be in a Church. The Ten Commandments are a very essential part of how peoples lives pan out. Though Shalt not steal springs to mind, sadly this Commandment is totally forgotten about when you look at the amount of stealing and fraud that goes on to-day, in all walks of life.

Housebreaking, Shoplifting, defrauding the benefits system, all different methods of stealing the list is endless.

The next commandment that springs to mind is thou Shalt not Kill, open a news paper any day of the week and I'm almost certain there will be a paragraph relating to someone being killed unlawfully. When a person leaves their home and they are carrying an offensive weapon, they must be aware that if they use that weapon be it a knife or a gun the chances are that the victim will die. In my eyes that is premeditated murder and should be treated as such. But no, if the perpetrator pleads guilty, or to diminished responsibility he or she will be charged with manslaughter which carries a much lighter sentence. Why not an eye for an eye, a tooth for a tooth as quoted in the bible, when one human being snuffs out another human beings life they should receive the maximum sentence possible.

To sum up the problems we face in modern times, my personal opinion is that our Government has completely lost the plot. I'm not blaming it on the present Co-alition Government because they inherited a bag of worms. As I said previously we have lost all forms of discipline, how do we retrieve that,? I have wracked my brains and cant come up with any answers, the minute the government tries to impose new rules and regulations the do gooders will step in and block all forms of discipline with the backing of the EEC. I keep hearing the four wisemen, Cameron, Glegg, Alexander and Osborne saying they must get people off benefits and back to work. I wish they would tell the unemployed where the work is I'm sure some of them would be delighted to have a job.

This week in the press one headline stated that one hundred and sixty thousand jobs were filled with immigrants last year, it is time this was looked into and the influx of immigrants cut back drastically. The people on benefits should be forced to fill these jobs regardless of who they are.

The family unit where there is a competent mother and father bringing up the children is another area that is badly needing overhauling, it is stated many girls deliberately get pregnant so that they qualify for a house and higher benefits, there is also the booze culture, many children are conceived when the mother is drunk and has no idea who the father is. Another headache for any government to sort out.

Finally drugs the curse of our society, it would be interesting to know just how many people in this country are hooked on drugs, we are aware of the ones who are dependant on methadone because of the Government Statistics but there are so many different drugs abused it would be difficult to get an accurate figure. There is also the problem of alcohol abuse young people ruining their lives and leaving themselves with horrendous medical problems, and of course this all adds to the huge bill it costs the N.H.S to treat them, thus depriving people with genuine health problems from receiving treatment because of lack of funds.

The SNP are touting the date for a referendum to vote on the break-up of the U.K. Is this a wise move? We are not being told enough about the idea behind this move. My first question would be where is the funding going to come from, apart from Whisky and Tourism what else have we that generates a lot of income, then there are all the social problems I highlighted we have them in Scotland the same as everywhere else.

Up until now I would say Kenny MacAskill has shown to be quite a soft touch in his role as justice minister releasing prisoners when they are only a few months into their sentence. I can not see him making any significant changes to law and order in our country. Then Nicola Sturgeon minister for the NHS, she keeps insisting on budget cut backs in the NHS service but is she aware what goes on at the rock face. The NHS Hospitals Wards are being kept running because of the dedicated older Staff Nurses who received their training under a Matron, they are dedicated ladies who work well past the end of their shift to catch up with paperwork and reports, in most cases they don't get paid for the little favours they do the NHS, if they were to down tools at the end of their twelve hour day and go home the whole system would be in chaos. But Miss Sturgeon and her back up team will not be present at the beginning and end of the shift so probably know nothing of this small freebee's given by the dedicated nursing staff.

Where will all this turmoil end,? There seems to be no light at the end of the tunnel, my family are pretty lucky in as much as they all have jobs and they are reasonably safe. But you are never sure how things can change overnight, one of the problems as I see it, is that there is more emphasis on College and University training than there is in practical training, get in at the coal face and see how the big boys do it. First of all I personally would get pretty bored sitting in a class room listing to a lecturer talking about subjects I probably know very little about. At the end of three years or whatever, these people are let loose in jobs they have spent their time reading about in textbooks and writing essays. I think it is back to front, the training should be done on the job and by all means have the students in collage to sit exams so that their progress can be monitored, maybe I am old fashioned but I am entitled to my opinion.

The latest Press release highlights that the South Of Scotland Electricity Board are submitting plans for two huge Hydro Schemes in the heart of the Highlands, a six hundred megawatt scheme producing enough electricity to power quarter of a million homes this would be constructed at Balmacaan in Glen Urquhart. The second Scheme is being proposed at Core Glas near Laggan and Loch Lochy again this is a monster producing 600 MW of power.

Between these two sites there would be in the region of one thousand jobs plus the spin off work, but who will get the jobs?. The hundreds of unemployed Scots or will a Foreign Construction Company sneak in one thousand Eastern Europeans like they did in Glendoe. Our first Minister should make sure he looks after the Scots after and all he will be depending on a lot of Scots turning out to vote for him in the near future.

FULL OF THE JOYS OF SPRING

We are heading fast to the Spring of twenty thousand and twelve, the buds are appearing on the tree's and the spring flowers will soon burst into life. You would think we should have a new lease of life knowing that with-in a few months we will be enjoying summer sunshine. But I am afraid we are far from happy times. The financial situation is getting worse, unemployment at an all time high, what is there to be happy about when all around us is doom and gloom.

Very soon Scotland is to embark on building another huge bridge over the Firth Of Forth a massive under taking considering all the elements that will be against the bridge builders. When I speak about work, most of the time it is about the Construction Industry this is because most of my working life was spent in Civil/ Heavy Engineering so I feel fully qualified to speak about this field. The new Forth Bridge will create many hundreds of badly needed jobs, we should be glad as it will maybe shorten the dole queues. But which country's dole queues will it shorten? the reason I ask this question is that it was announced in the press last week that all of the thirty six thousand ton's of steel required to build the bridge has already been sourced and that no British Company had been considered when the contracts were placed. This is bloody well scandalous, who sanctions this travesty and sneakily goes about placing work abroad that can easily be done in Britain, it's just not good enough. What is the problem are the British Manufacturers too costly,? It looks like it when our government are prepared to go to places like China ahead of our own work forces. This must have been known about for quite some time as it is quite a protracted and complex procedure to produce steel. Many tests have to be carried out too make sure the steel is strong enough to withstand the rigours of what it is to be used for, things like weather, the items it will be needed to support so it's a pretty thorough procedure before it is accepted as the finished article, not like making a pot of soup. I presume as many of the components possible, will be made on shore and shipped to the work site again this should provide much needed work, this could be done in Fife or the Clyde Ship yards, but in my mind we are very close to Spain who have many facilities capable of doing this kind of work cheaper than it can be done in the U.K, but it will be sinful if this were to happen. Reading the latest Press Release the awarding of the contracts are all done and dusted with Scotland being awarded less than twenty percent of the work. This doesn't include the Construction of the Bridge it will be interesting to see who is awarded that contract and what nationality the Labour Force will be. With the state the whole of the United Kingdom finds its self in surly the emphasis should have been made on securing as many jobs as possible twenty percent is just a handful of crumbs as far as I am concerned enough to keep the natives happy.

If this had been in France or many of the other E.U countries the whole place would have been crippled by the workforce going on strike standing up for their rites. Where are all our highly overpaid Union Officials' when the British Government are allowing British Work to be done in countries that are inferior to the UK?.

THE END

Lightning Source UK Ltd.
Milton Keynes UK
UKOW050051180512

192789UK00001B/248/P